Mel Bay Presents

JAZZ CELLO/BASS WIZARD

Junior, Book 2

by Martin Norgaard

The rhythm section on the CD is: Bruce Dudley (Piano) • Charlie Chadwick (Bass) • Jim White (Drums)

1 2 3 4 5 6 7 8 9 0

Visit us on the Web at www.melbay.com — E-mail us at email@melbay.com

INTRODUCTION

Jazz Cello/Bass Wizard Junior 2 is a continuation of *Jazz Cello Wizard Junior* (20189BCD Mel Bay, 2002) and is designed for upper middle school and high school string students. *JCWjr 2* uses the same basic approach as JCWjr; students learn mainly through imitation, the same way we learn to speak our native tongue. It also introduces very easy optional chord theory but only AFTER the student has experienced improvising with chords aurally. The books come in three versions—violin, viola, and cello/bass—which are identical except for clefs and register; they are designed to be used together in studio and classroom situations. For advanced high school and college violin students, the original *Jazz Fiddle Wizard* (98379BCD Mel Bay, 2000) is also applicable.

In addition to the continuing focus on rhythm, this volume introduces three basic concepts that are prerequisites to advanced jazz improvising: solo development, modes, and inner melodies. Solo development is the ability to "tell a story" in your improvisation—essential for connecting with your audience. Learning modes shows students that the finger patterns they already know can be used to create new scales such as Aeolian and Mixolydian. Most importantly, this volume introduces inner melodies, an innovative way of teaching improvisation on non-diatonic chord progressions. It focuses the student on the guiding notes that improvisers use to maneuver through changing chords. The goal is for students to be able to audiate (hear inside their heads) inner melodies even as they improvise around them. This concept helps students experience the "big picture" before delving into details. I have found inner melodies to be the single most potent technique to get students to improvise on advanced progressions immediately.

JCWjr 2 contains five lessons and four tunes and includes bass parts for all compositions (though the theory behind bassline construction is left out because it is covered in numerous bass instruction books). The original format of dividing performance pieces into lines A, B, and C is retained for maximum flexibility of instrumentation. I recommend in a string orchestra performance that the violins play line A, violas line B, cellos line C, and basses the bass part. Though a live rhythm section is preferable in an orchestra setting (have the drummer learn the part off the CD and ask the pianist to disregard the left hand in the rehearsal piano part), I have successfully used the CD as background in chamber concerts using a boom box placed right behind the group. Since line A was designed as a violin part, be aware it reaches into the higher registers in the viola and cello books.

I am eager to get feedback on this and other books in the series. Please email me and let me know how the books worked in your setting.

Martin Norgaard, June 2004
Martin@JazzFiddleWizard.com

WEBSITE

Visit www.JazzFiddleWizard.com for information on the history of jazz strings, a comprehensive discography, lesson plans, assessment tools, and course syllabi. Hear rare recordings of jazz violinists on the JazzFiddleWizard.com radio station.

ACKNOWLEDGMENTS

Thanks to my improvisation students at the University of Texas at Austin String Project and the South Carolina Suzuki Institute for helping me test this book. A special thanks to the String Project director, Dr. Laurie Scott. Also thanks to Renata Bratt and Utah Hamrick for help with the cello/bass edition. My sincerest gratitude to my editor, Laura Reed, who has helped shape the entire junior series.

TABLE OF CONTENTS

LESSON 1:
QUESTION AND ANSWER PHRASES

Improvising can be compared to talking. In Book 1 of this series, we explored how to talk with other musicians using rhythm and melody. In this lesson we'll explore how starting and ending on specific notes makes the phrase sound like a question or an answer. All eighth notes are played with a swing feel. Though most jazz bass (and even many jazz cello solos) are played pizzicato, the exercises throughout this book can be done either pizzicato or arco.

Track # 1: Tuning note A

Track # 2: We start in G major (the same key we used in Lesson 3 of Book 1). First let's just review the scale. You can use Track # 9 to practice a full two-octave scale.

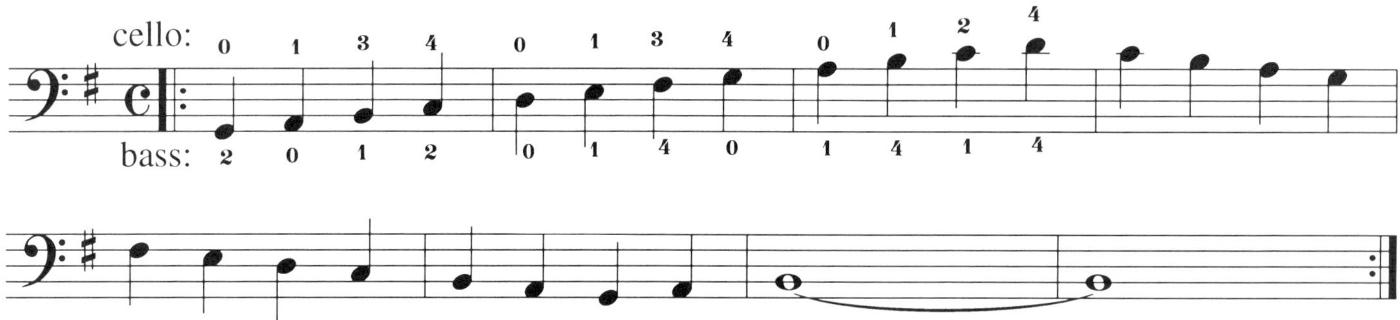

Track # 3: We assign numbers to the notes in the scale so they can be referred to easily. The key is named after scale degree 1, also called the root. When we get past 7, we start over with the second octave. Say the numbers as you play the scale slowly:

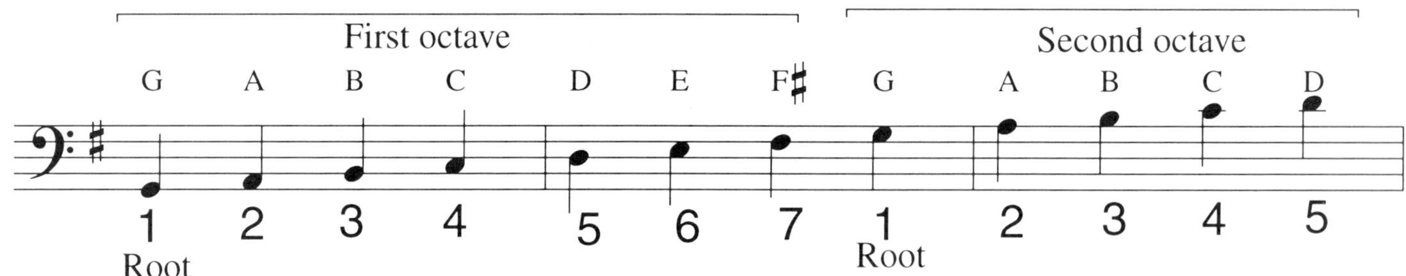

Games (not on CD): Call out a scale-step number and see if the students can match a pitch to the number. You can also use visual hand signals to communicate melodies by having students in a class match pitch according to the number of fingers (1 through 7) displayed.

(Teacher: The relationship between numbers and notes is equivalent to solfege with movable Do. Other books are available on this subject so we return to our goal of developing improvisation skills.)

Track # 4: Let's play some questions and answers that start on specific notes. Improvise a short answer phrase that starts on the same note as the question phrase on the CD. The tiny notes below are just suggestions; make up your own lick. (See JCWjr Book 1 for more on the principle of repeating and answering a "musical question.")

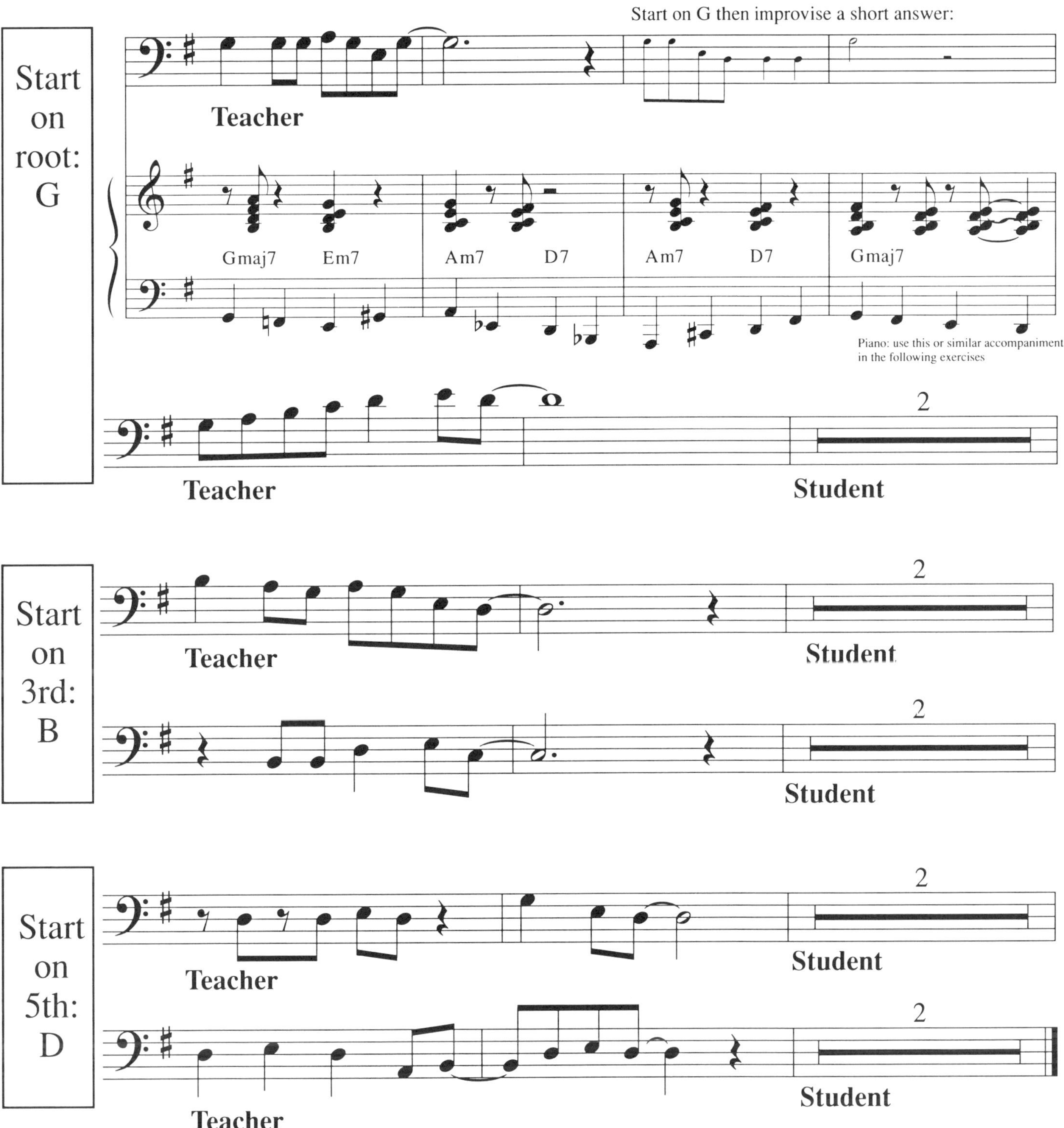

Notice that when we emphasized the root in the previous exercise it sounded "heavy" as if we were ending the conversation. In other words, the phrase sounds like a question when it does NOT end on the root, and it sounds like an answer when it ends on the root. In the following exercises we alternate between two types of phrases. The first question phrase starts and ends on a note other than the root. The second answer phrase starts and ends on the root G.

Track # 5: First answer the CD by improvising answer phrases that start and end on the root. (The CD uses a couple of chromatic approach notes. You'll learn about those in Book 3.)

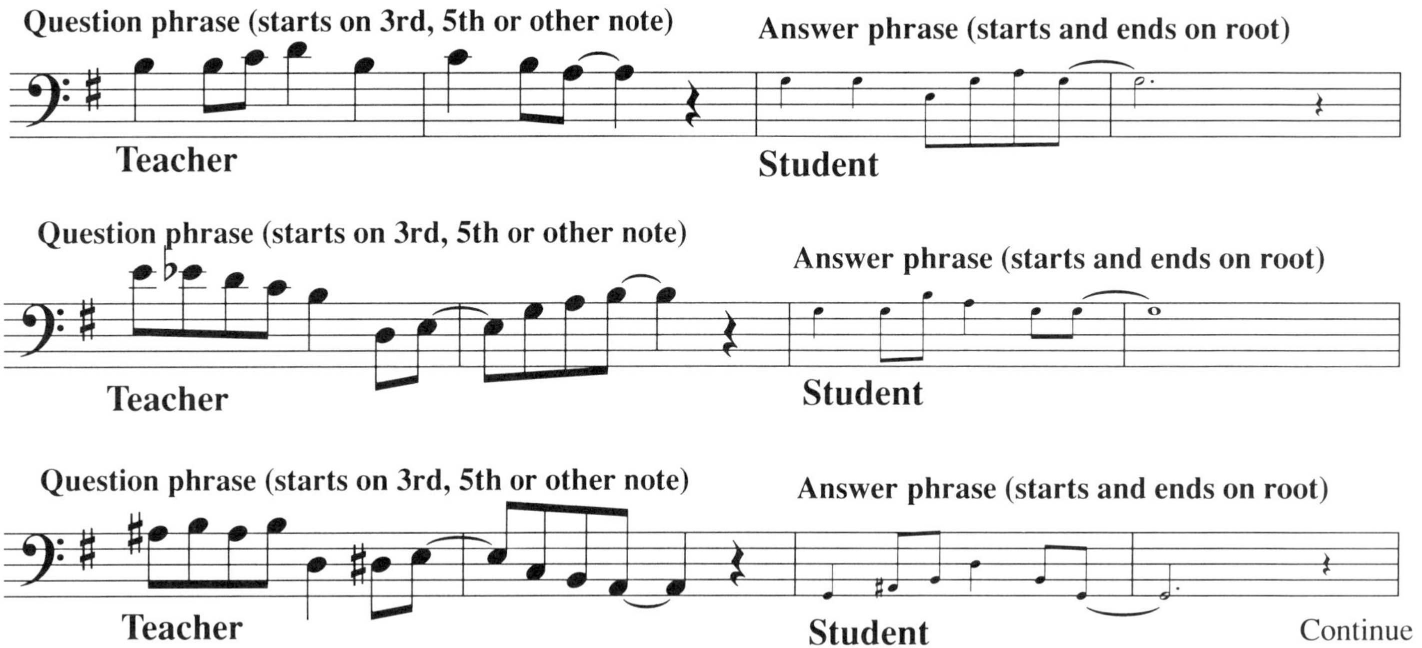

Track # 6: Now you ask the question by playing a short phrase that doesn't start or end on the root (start on 3rd, 5th or another note), and the CD will answer. In other words: YOU START!

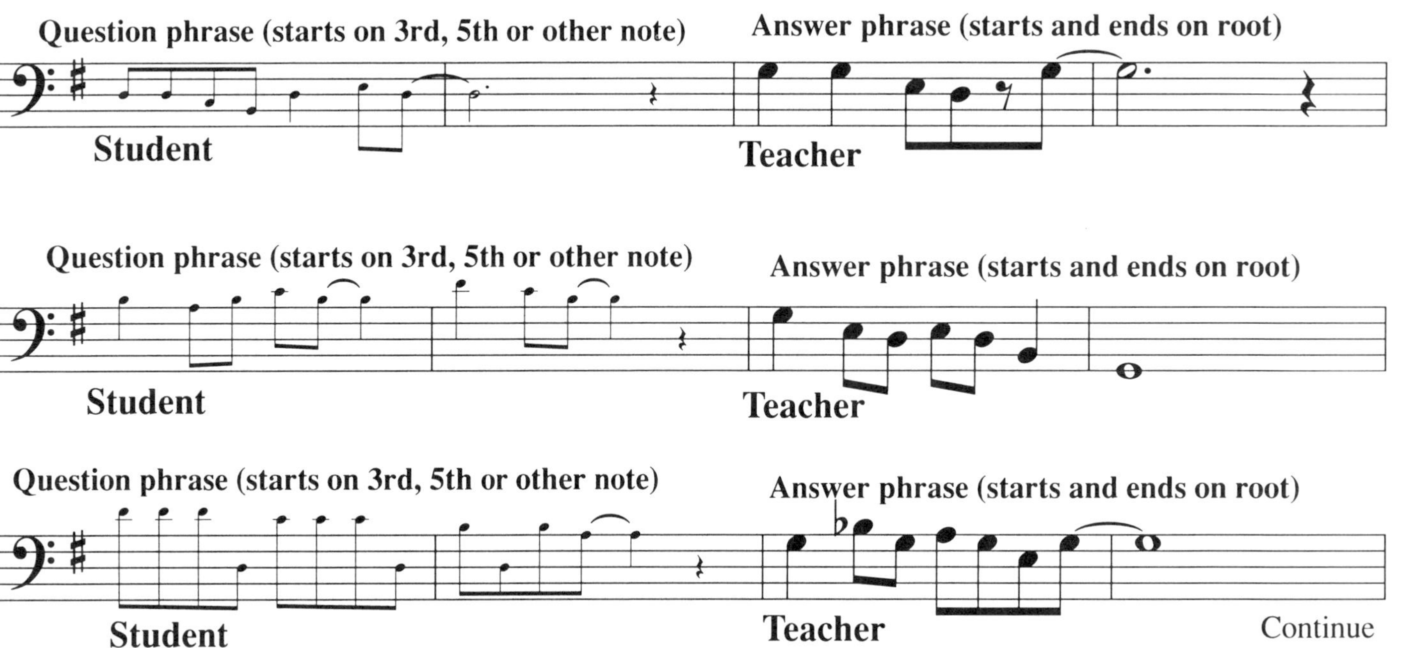

Track # 7: You should now be able to alternate between question and answer phrases within your own solo by emphasizing different notes. After the CD plays a sample, try it yourself. The small G notes in the last two measures are included to help you remember to emphasize G in your improvisation.

(Teacher: In a classroom setting, split the students into two groups; one plays question licks [start on 3rd or 5th or any other note] and the other plays answer licks [start and end on root]. Then alternate between individuals from each group using Track # 9 [backup only].)

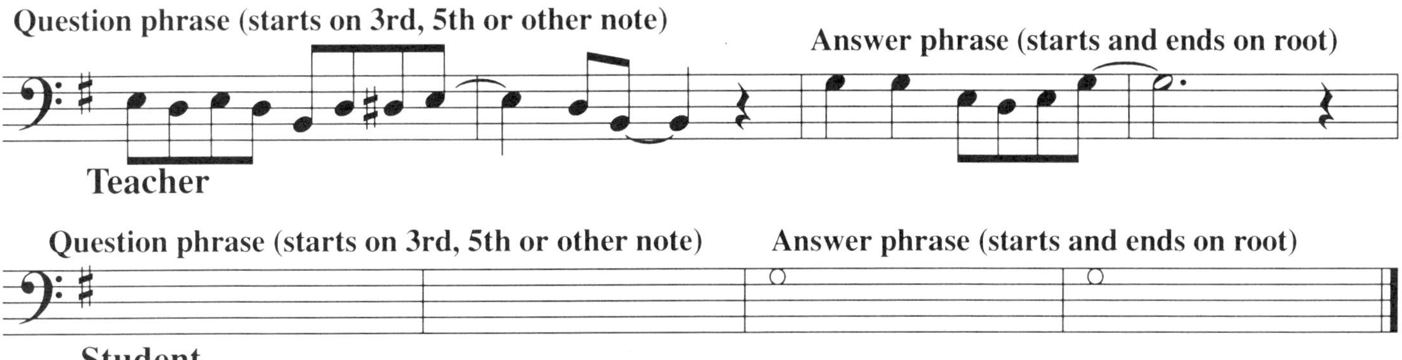

Track # 8: What if you want to elaborate on your question before the answer? In other words, if you improvise a longer solo, you may want to stay away from the root until the end of your solo. Play along with the example below then improvise your own solo. Notice how I emphasize the root in measures 7 and 8 to give my solo a sense of closure. The drums on the backup track help by playing a particular drum lick every eight measures.

(Teacher: If practicing this exercise to piano accompaniment, use the solo section from "Turnaround Town.")

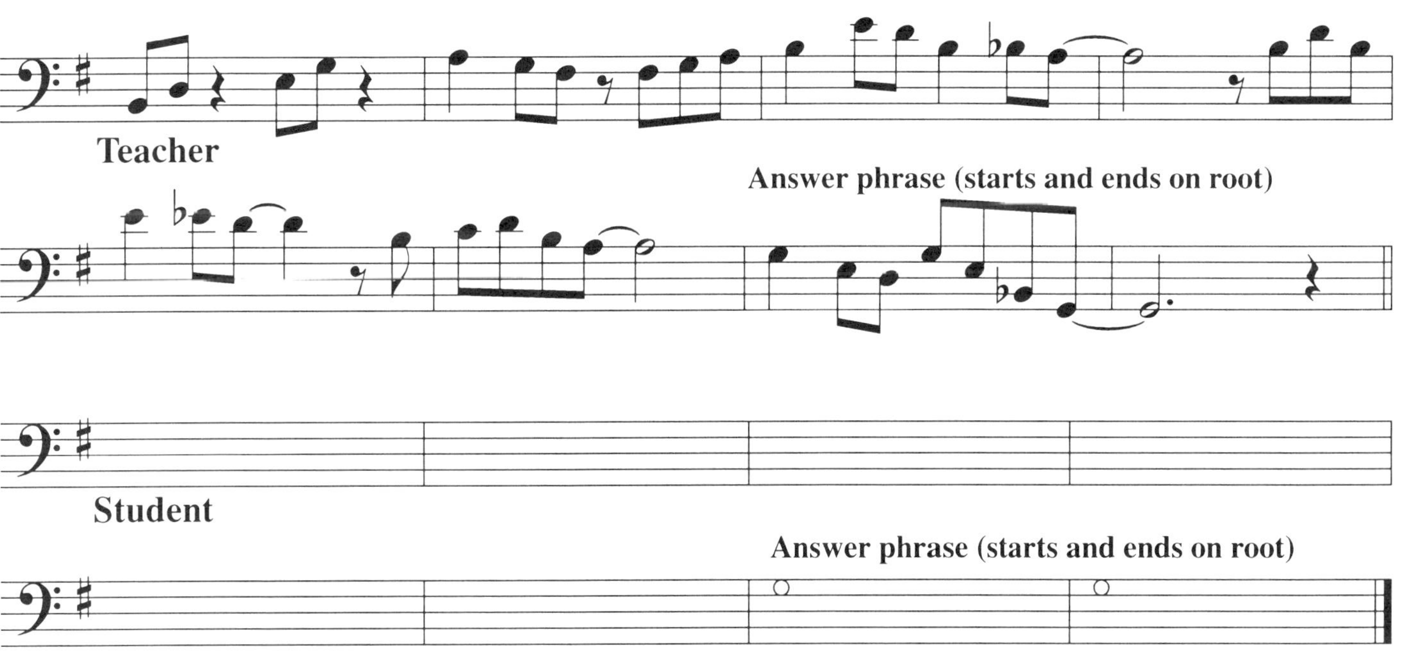

Track # 9: This track contains rhythm section only. Try playing several eight-measure solos ending each on the note G. In a larger group, let each member try an eight-measure solo.

(Teacher: It is very important to start each solo at the beginning of an eight-measure phrase as clearly marked by the rhythm section.)

LESSON 2:
TELLING A STORY

In Lesson 1 we learned that starting and ending on different notes affects how the phrase feels and functions. In this lesson we'll look at how speed and register in a single phrase relates to the full solo.

Register: Playing in the low register makes the phrase sound low in energy, while playing in a higher register raises the energy level.

Track # 10: Using the same scale as in Lesson 1, G major, improvise answers in the same register as the CD's question phrases. Don't worry about beginning and ending on a particular note for now. The teacher phrases on the CD are played on violin and therefore do not go below G but go higher than your regular register. You should use your C (cello) or E (bass) strings in you low register answers. (Teacher: The following exercises use the same piano accompaniment as Lesson 1.)

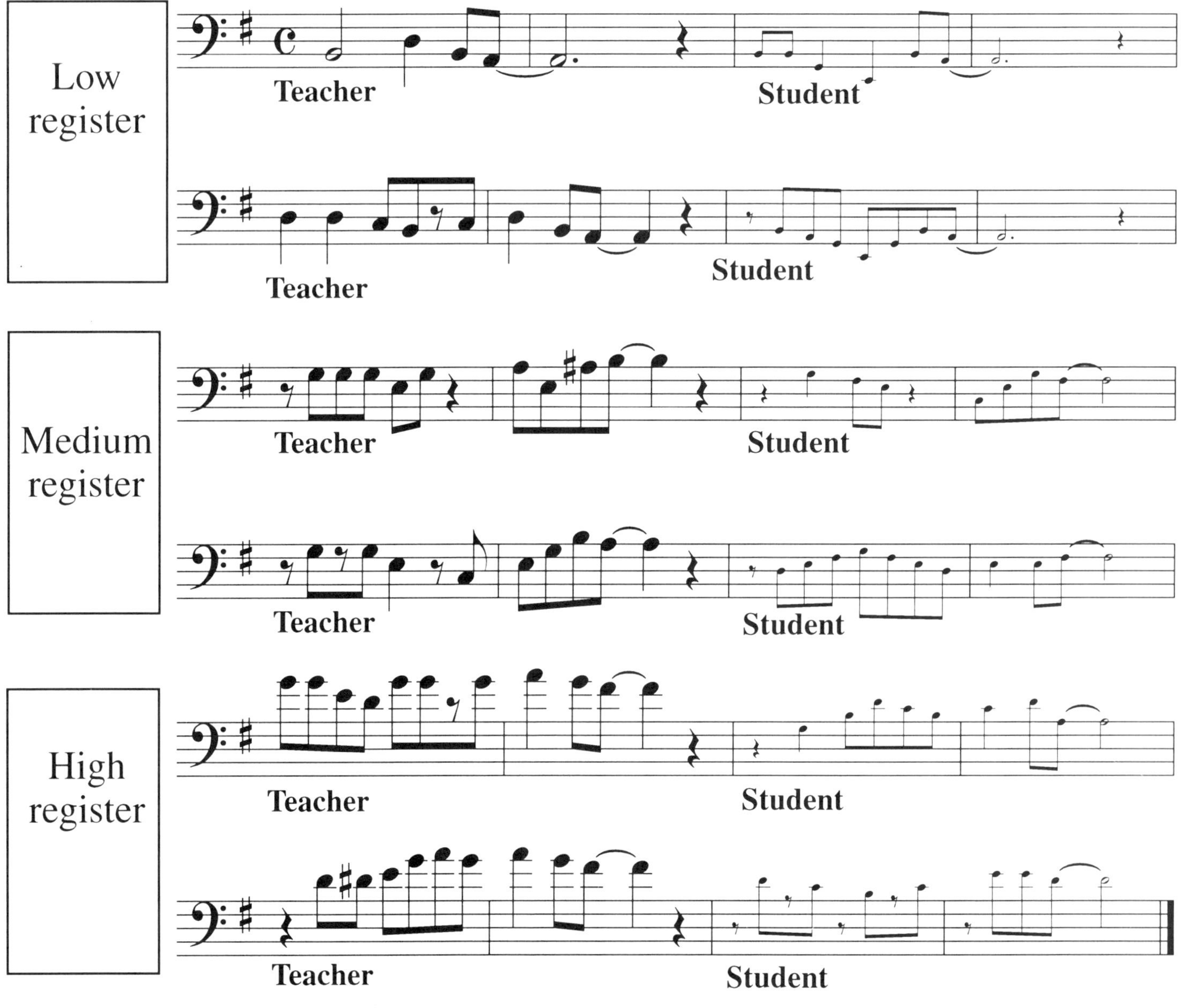

To tell a story in your solo, try starting with low energy phrases then build by playing in a higher and higher register. Toward the end return to the lower register and finish the solo with an answer phrase that emphasizes the root, as we learned in Lesson 1. Below is a diagram that represents energy over the course of the solo:

How to tell a story:

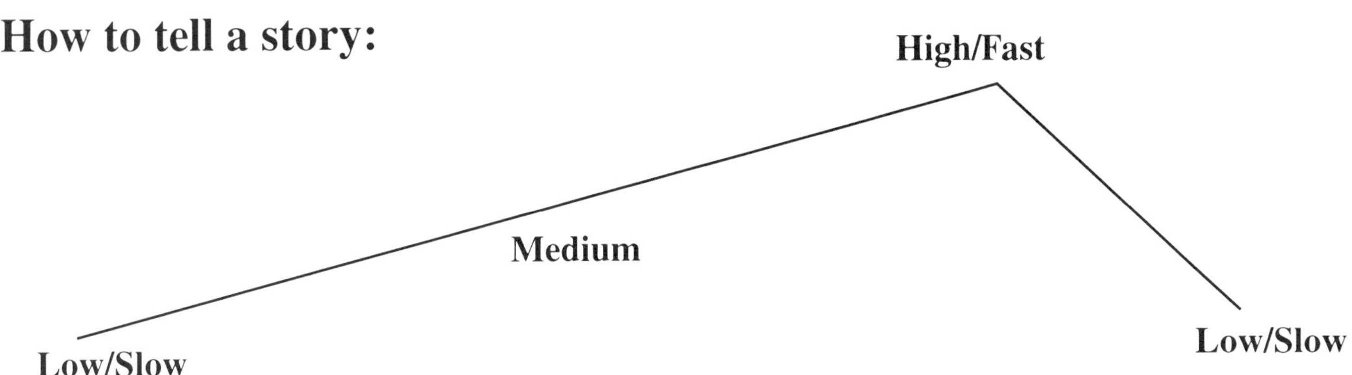

Track # 11: Now try to organize the phrases in an eight-bar solo so they follow this form. Listen and follow along with the violin sample (notated an octave down) then improvise your own solo while trying to vary your register. (Teacher: Use the piano accompaniment from the solo section of "Turnaround Town.")

Space & Speed: On the "how to tell a story" diagram, notice that speed (fast/slow) is also listed as a factor. Speed here refers to rhythm; the tempo of the music does not change. The faster rhythms you play and the less space between notes, the more energy the phrase has.

Track # 12: Improvise answer phrases using approximately the same speed or note values as the question phrase:

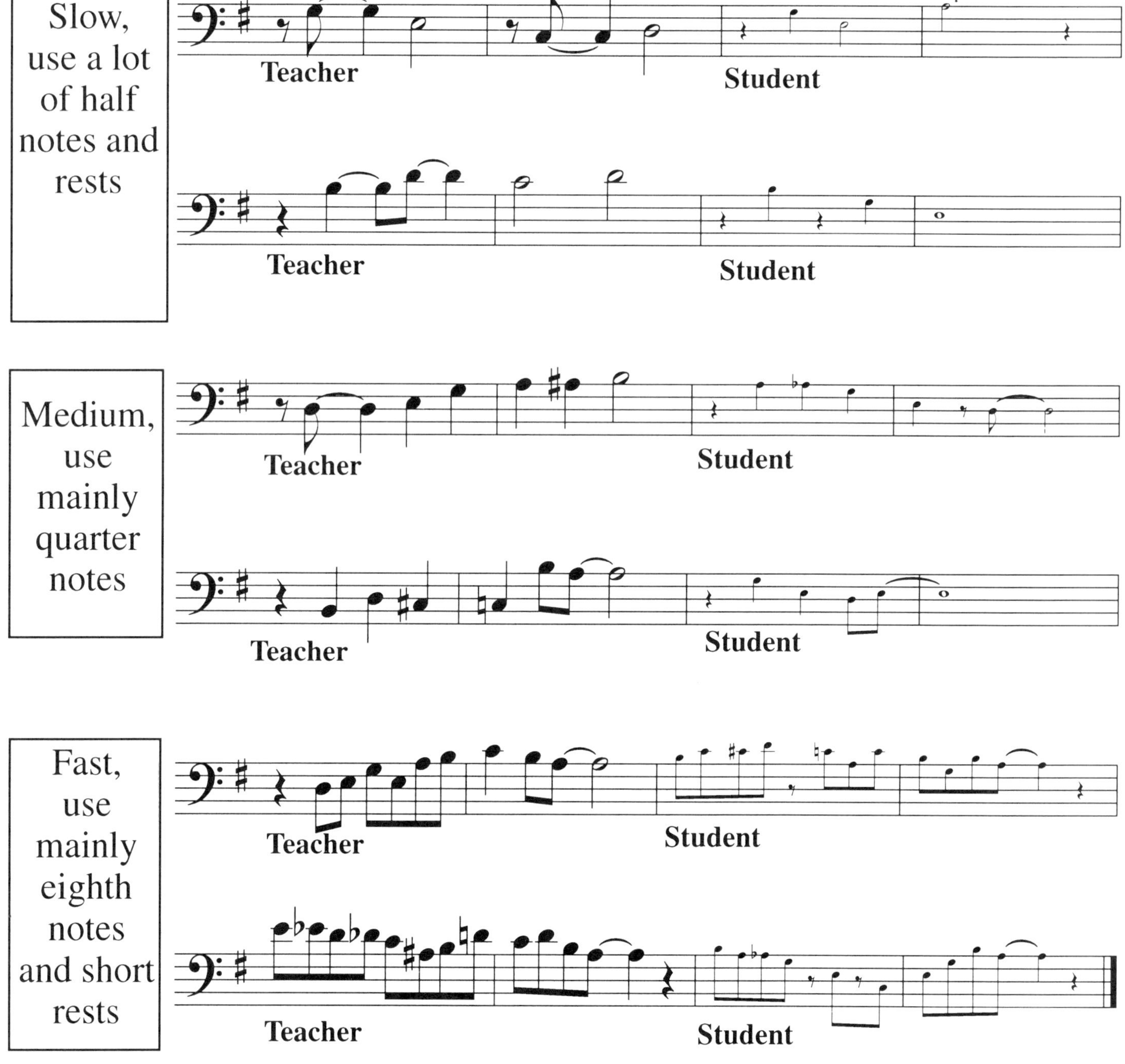

Track # 13: Now let's see if we can organize our phrases according to speed and space: start slowly with a lot of rests, then get faster and faster eliminating rests. Finally end slowly with a phrase ending on G. Listen or play with the sample, then try it yourself:

Track # 14: Finally, try to combine both story-telling devices to create a solo form that really makes the audience listen. Start slowly in a low register, then play higher and faster, ending slowly on the low G. Listen first, then try yourself. Use Track # 9 (backup only) to try this many times or in a larger group. You are now ready to improvise the solo in "Turnaround Town":

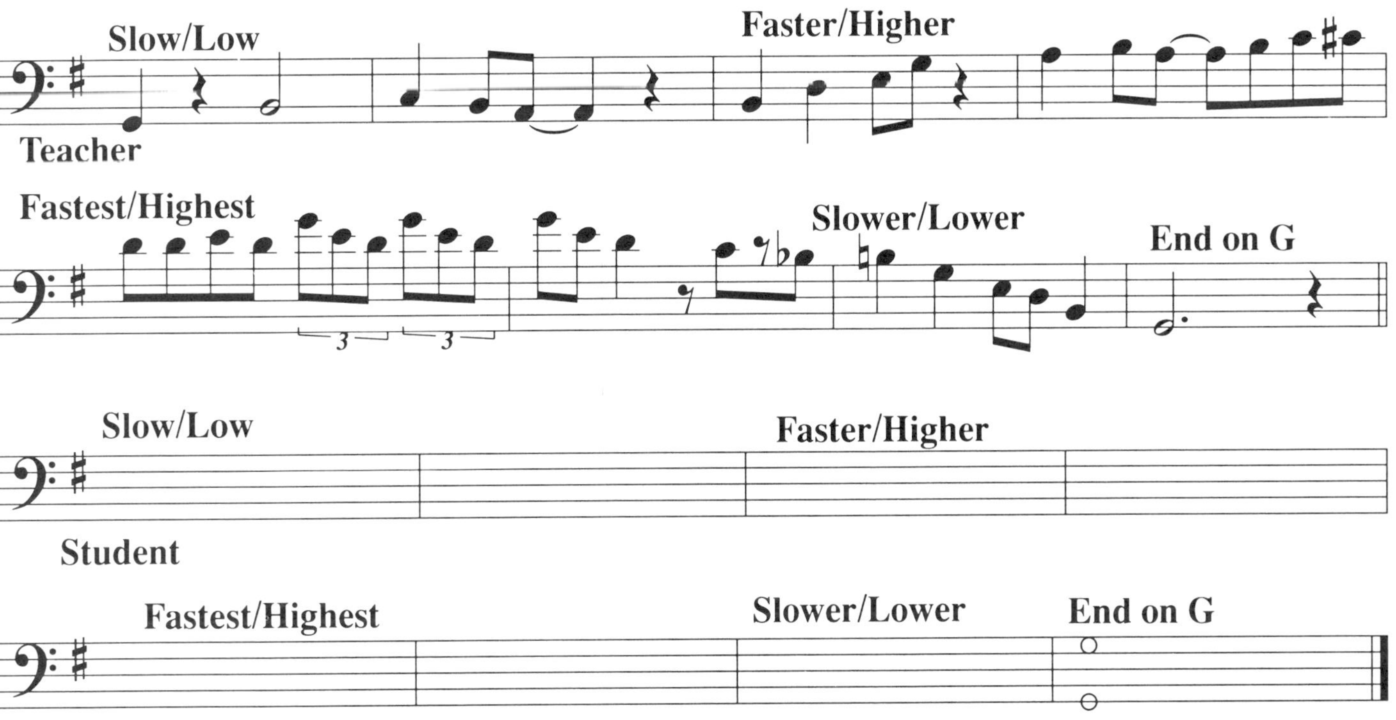

Line A

TURNAROUND TOWN

15 & 16

Line B

TURNAROUND TOWN

Cello
(Line C)

TURNAROUND TOWN

Bass

15 & 16

TURNAROUND TOWN

Light Swing ♩= 115

M. Norgaard

pizz. *mf*

Am7 | Am7 D7 | Bm7 | Bm7 E7 | Am7 Bm7 | Cmaj7 D7 G

7 D7 | [9] Gmaj7 Em7 *mf* | Am7 D7 | Bm7 Em7 | Dm7 G7

13 Cmaj7 | Cm7 F7 | B♭maj7 | Am7 D7 | [17] Gmaj7 Em7 | Am7 D7

19 Bm7 Em7 | Dm7 G7 | Cmaj7 | Cm7 F7 | Am7 | B7

[25] 𝄋 Em7 *p* | C7 | Em7 | A7 | Dm7 | B♭7

31 Bm7 E7 | Am7 D7 | [33] Gmaj7 Em7 *mf* | Am7 D7 | Bm7 Em7 | Dm7 G7

37 Cmaj7 | Cm7 F7 | B♭maj7 | E7♭9 | Am7 | Am7 D7

43 Bm7 | Bm7 E7 | Am7 Bm7 | Cmaj7 D7 G 𝄌 | D7

Solos

49 Gmaj7 Em7 | Am7 D7 | Gmaj7 Em7 | Am7 D7 | Gmaj7 Em7 | Am7 D7

55 Am7 D7 | 1.2.3. Gmaj7 D7 | 4. Gmaj7 B7

D.S. al Coda

𝄌

TURNAROUND TOWN

Light Swing ♩= 115

M. Norgaard

10
A
B
C
Am7 D7 Bm7 Em7 Dm7 G7 Cmaj7 Cm7 F7
Bass
10
Am7 D7 Bm7 Em7 Dm7 G7 Cmaj7 Cm7 F7
Pia.

15
17
A
B
C
B♭maj7 Am7 D7 Gmaj7 Em7 Am7 D7 Bm7 Em7
Bass
15
B♭maj7 Am7 D7 17 Gmaj7 Em7 Am7 D7 Bm7 Em7
Pia.

20
A
B
C
Dm7 G7 Cmaj7 Cm7 F7 Am7 B7
Bass
Dm7 G7 Cmaj7 Cm7 F7 Am7 B7
20
Pia.

25
A
p
B
C
Em7 C7 Em7 A7 Dm7
Bass
25
Em7 C7 Em7 A7 Dm7
p
Pia.

30
A
B
C
Bass
Pia.
33
vln
vla
mf
B♭7 Bm7 E7 Am7 D7 Gmaj7 Em7 Am7 D7

35
A
B
C
Bass
Pia.
Bm7 Em7 Dm7 G7 Cmaj7 Cm7 F7 B♭maj7

40
A
B
C
arco
E7♭9
Am7
Am7 D7
Bm7
Bm7 E7
Bass
40
E7♭9
Am7
Am7 D7
Bm7
Bm7 E7
Pia.

45
A
Solos
Gmaj7
Em7
B
Solos
Gmaj7
Em7
C
Solos
Gmaj7
Em7
Am7
Bm7
Cmaj7
D7
G
D7
pizz.
Solos
Gmaj7
Em7
Bass
Am7
Bm7
Cmaj7
D7
G
D7
Solos
Gmaj7
Em7
45
Pia.

50
A
B
C
Bass
Pia.
Am7 D7 Gmaj7 Em7 Am7 D7 Gmaj7 Em7 Am7 D7

55
A
B
C
Bass
Pia.
Am7 D7
1.2.3. Gmaj7 D7
4. Gmaj7 B7
D.S. al Coda

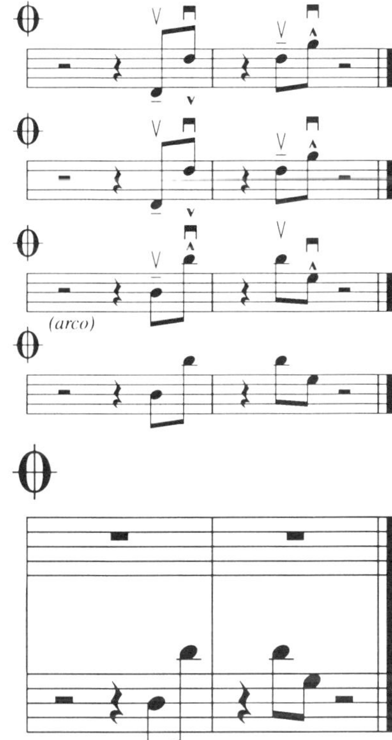
(arco)

LESSON 3:
INNER MELODIES

In Lesson 1 we discovered that ending on the root gave the phrase a sense of closure. In this lesson we'll look at what happens before we get to the root. Just as emphasizing the root in the last measure made sense in our improvisation, we can emphasize other notes in other measures. These guiding notes form a melody that the listener doesn't necessarily hear because we improvise around it. We call it an Inner Melody. In the advanced section, students will learn that the inner melody is derived from the chord notes in the accompaniment.

The rhythm in this lesson and the following piece is a light Latin feel, meaning that we don't swing the eighth notes as we did in the previous two lessons.

Track # 17: First we simply play the inner melody. You can play it in whatever octave you like. Notice the inner melody is both notated and listed inside the circles above the measures. (Teacher: If you are using piano instead of the CD, here is an accompaniment that works on all the exercises in this lesson.)

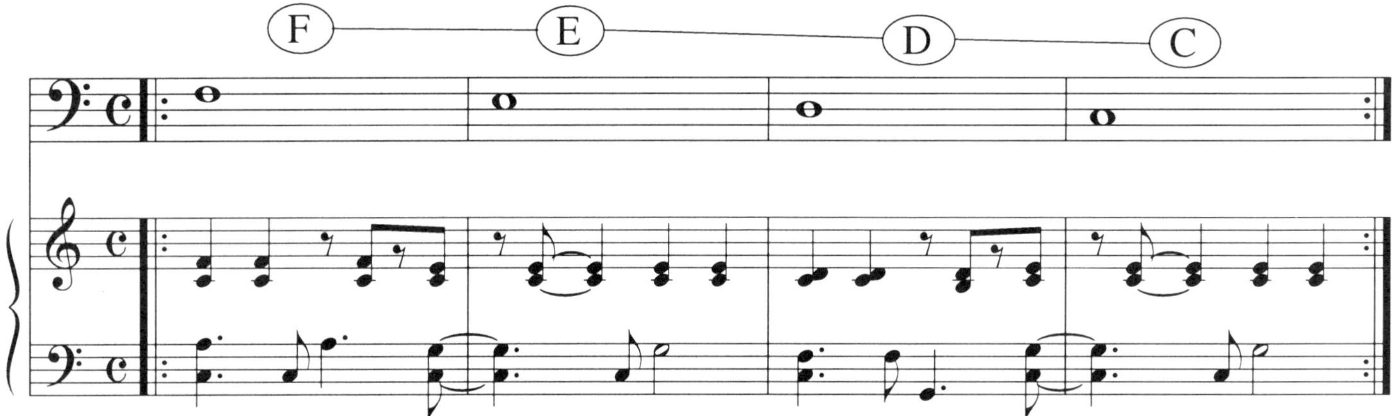

Track # 18: Now we add rhythms to the inner melody. Try to do this by ear as you listen to the CD. You know the melody; catch the rhythm when you can. Play the eighth notes as precisely and evenly as you can:

Continue

Track # 19: Now add your own rhythms to the inner melody line. You don't have to play the same rhythm in each measure. Play along with the sample then try it yourself. The inner melody is now listed as small round notes in your music to remind you to play a rhythm based on the notes written.

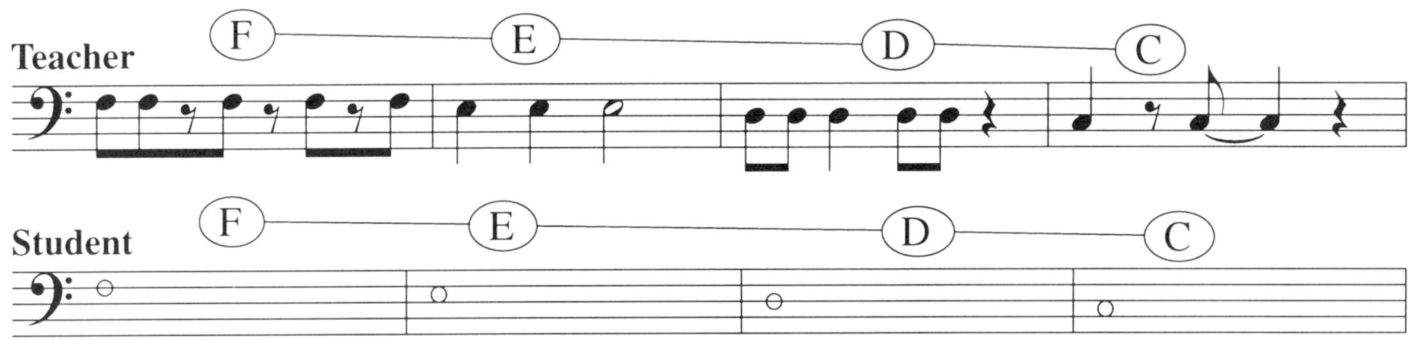

Continue

Track # 20: This time embellish the inner melody with other notes from the key of C. In the beginning, just ornament the inner melody. Later you can even try to jump between octaves if you feel adventurous. Listen to the sample phrases on the CD. (Teacher: In a group setting, have the rest of the group play the inner melody continuously in whole notes as individual students solo by embellishing the inner melody. Use Track # 22 [backup only].)

Teacher
F E D C

Student
F E D C

Teacher
F E D C

Student
F E D C

Teacher
F E D C

Student
F E D C

Continue

Track # 21: This lesson prepares you for the solo in "Northern Light." The solo is sixteen measures long and features a four-measure chord progression, repeated four times, that fits our inner melody. In other words, we play our inner melody four times in each solo. Here is an example that uses the inner melody freely combined with the story-telling devices we learned in the first two lessons. Notice that it starts slowly in a low register, develops to a higher register using faster notes, and ends slowly on the low root. The advanced lesson on the next page demonstrates how to find other inner melodies.

Track # 22: Now try it yourself. The track repeats the 16-measure progression many times, so you can try your solo many times or with members in a group. The ultimate goal is to hear the inner melody in your head while you drift away from it in your solo.

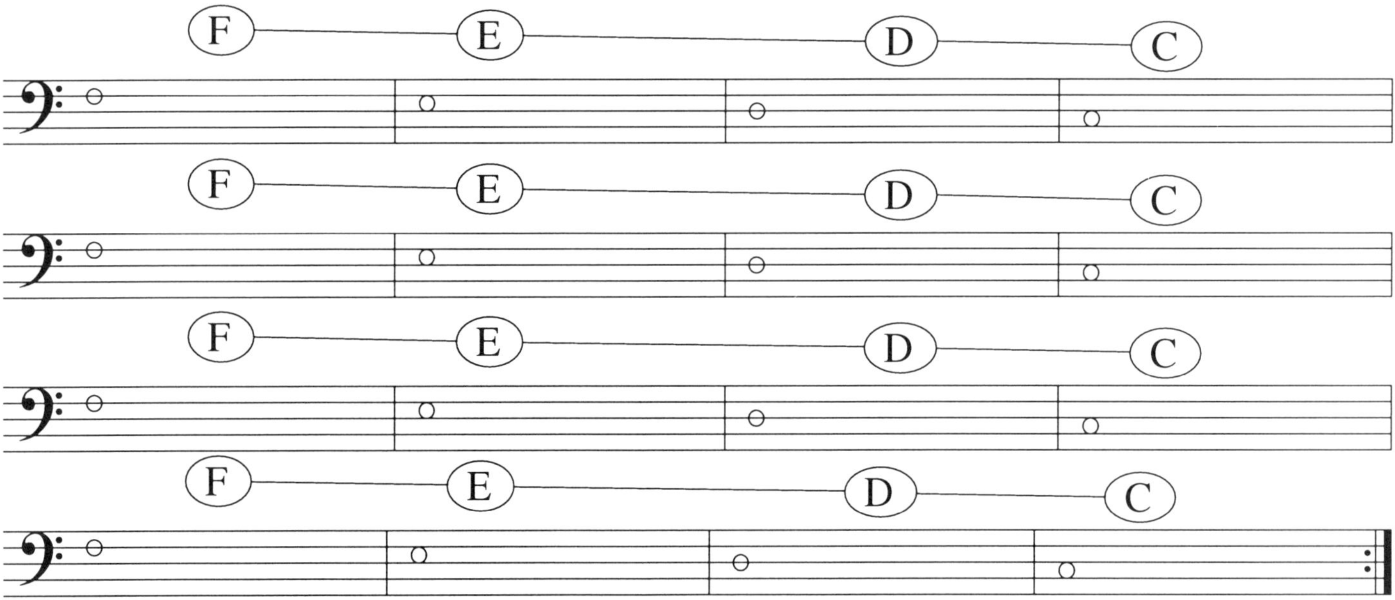

LESSON 3 (ADVANCED): HOW DID WE FIND THE INNER MELODY?

The following is for advanced students who have been introduced to basic music theory. The solo in "Northern Light" can easily be played without understanding the material below.

An inner melody is made up of individual chord tones that form a melody line.

The simplest inner melodies are often the chord tones closest together, and frequently they form an ascending or descending line. To find inner melodies we look at the chord structure of the accompaniment. The four-measure repeated figure that the solo in "Northern Light" is built on consists of chords with a pedal bassline figure. For now we will disregard the pedal bassline and simply look at the actual chords:

F C G7 C

Notice the chord symbols are just letters, while the inner melody is marked with circles and connected with lines. Notice the F (the root of the F triad) is only a half step away from the E (the 3rd of the C triad). The E goes to the D (5th of the G triad) then to the root of the C triad:

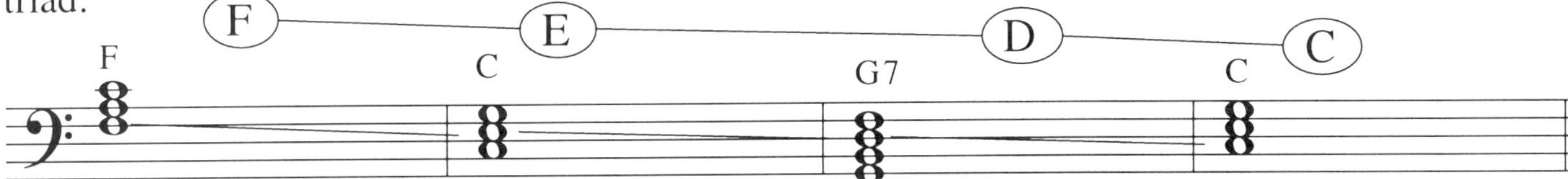

To find all possible inner melodies it is helpful to list the chords in multiple octaves.

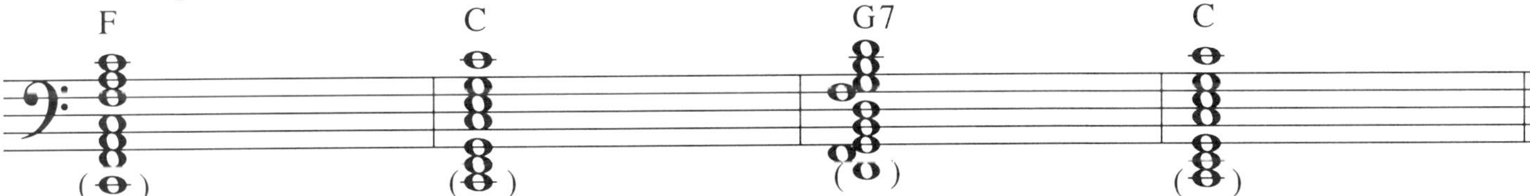

Here is another stepwise line:

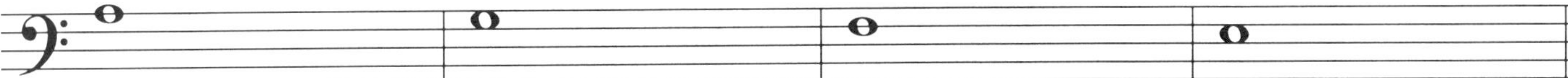

This one jumps around:

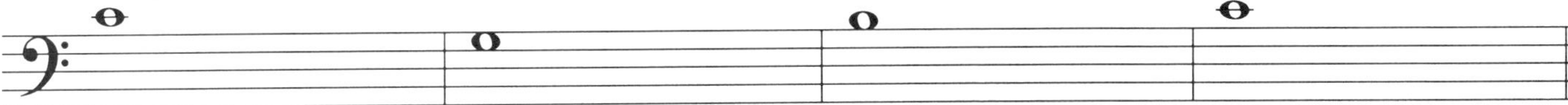

Written Exercise: Make up your own inner melody and play a solo to Track # 22 using the new inner melody as your guide. Make sure each measure contains a note from the chords above.

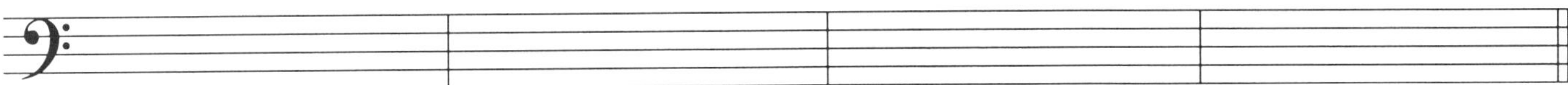

Line A

NORTHERN LIGHT

23 & 24

Light Latin
(even eighth) 𝅗𝅥 = 70

M. Norgaard

Cello opt.

mf

8

16 17 8 25

f

29 33

mf

35

42

Solos (write your inner melody in the circles)

49 F C G7 C F C G7 C

57 F C G7 C F C G7

64 C Interlude

f

(CD repeats solo 4 times)

Last time D.S. al Coda with repeats

69

rit.

mp

Line B

NORTHERN LIGHT

Light Latin
(even eighth) 𝅗𝅥 = 70

M. Norgaard

Cello opt.

mf

8

15

17

mp

22

25

29

33

mf

36

43

Solos (write your inner melody in the circles)

49 F C G7 C F C G7 C

57 F C G7 C F C G7

64 C

Interlude

f

(CD repeats solo 4 times)

Last time D.S. al Coda with repeats

69

rit.

mp

Cello
(Line C)

NORTHERN LIGHT

Bass

23 & 24

NORTHERN LIGHT

Light Latin
(even eighth) 𝅗𝅥 = 70

M. Norgaard

Am G Fmaj7 C/E
mf pizz.

9 Dm7 C/E F G

17 F/C C Gsus/C G C F/C C Gsus G C
mp

25 𝄋 F/C C Gsus/C G C F/C C Gsus G C

33 Am G Fmaj7 C/E
mf

41 Dm7 C/E 𝄌 F G

Solos
49 F/C C Gsus/C G C F/C C Gsus G

56 C F/C C Gsus/C G C F/C C

63 Gsus G C
Interlude
Am E/G♯ Gm D/F♯ F G
f
(CD repeats solo 4 times)
Last time D.S. al Coda with repeats

𝄌
69 F G Am Dm7 G7 Csus C
rit.
mp

 23 & 24

NORTHERN LIGHT

Light Latin (even eighth) ♩= 70

M. Norgaard

Line A
Line B
Line C
Bass
Piano

mf pizz.

Am G Fmaj7

Bdim/A Am Gsus G Fmaj7

A B C Bass Pia.

C/E Dm7

C/E F G

A
B
C
Bass
Pia.
17
F/C
C
Gsus/C
G
C
mp
25
f

A
B
C
Bass
Pia.
Gsus
G
C
33
mf
Am
B dim
A
Fmaj7
C
E
Dm7
F

Solos
F (write your inner melody in the circles)
A
B
C
Bass
Pia.
G7
C
F
Gsus
G

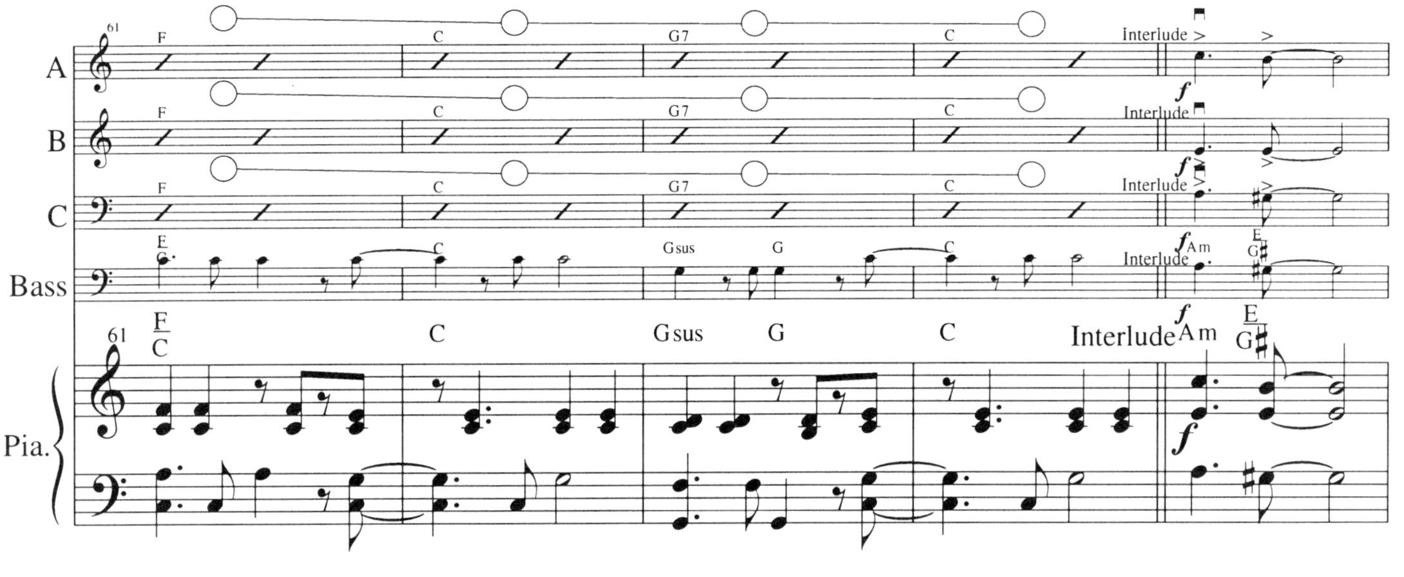

61
A
B
C
Bass
Pia.
F
C
G7
E/C
Gsus
G
Interlude
Am
E/G♯

66
A
B
C
Bass
Pia.
Gm
D/F♯
F
G
(CD repeats solo 4 times)
Last time D.S. al Coda with repeats

72
A
B
C
Bass
Pia.
Am
rit.
mp
Dm7
G7
Csus
C

LESSON 4:
CHANGING SCALES USING INNER MELODIES

In this lesson we will revisit the blues progression used in the tune "Wizard Blues" from Book 1. The blues progression was simplified so the same scale (D minor pentatonic) would work on all chords. This time, we use the inner melody technique from Lesson 3 to change between two scales (D Mixolydian and G Mixolydian) within the blues. You will find that inner melodies facilitate the changing between scales.

Track # 25: The blues consists of a twelve-bar form divided into three lines of four measures each. Here is the inner melody. Play along:

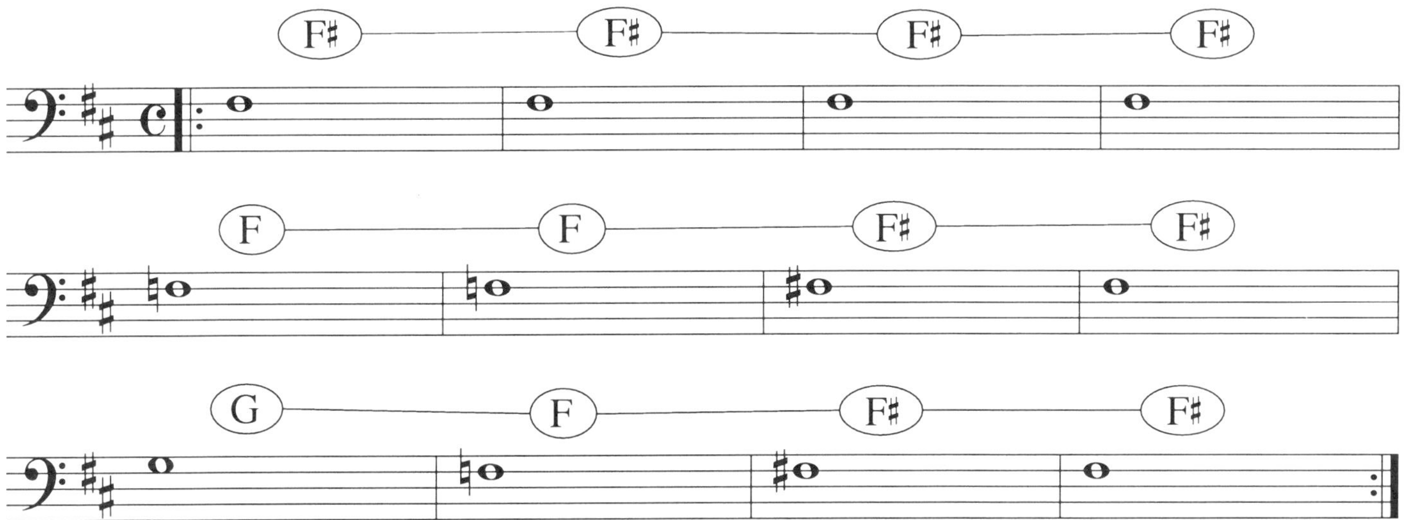

Track # 26: Let's play the inner melody with rhythms. Play the written rhythm in the first chorus and the rhythm on the CD in the next chorus by ear. Later make up your own rhythms.

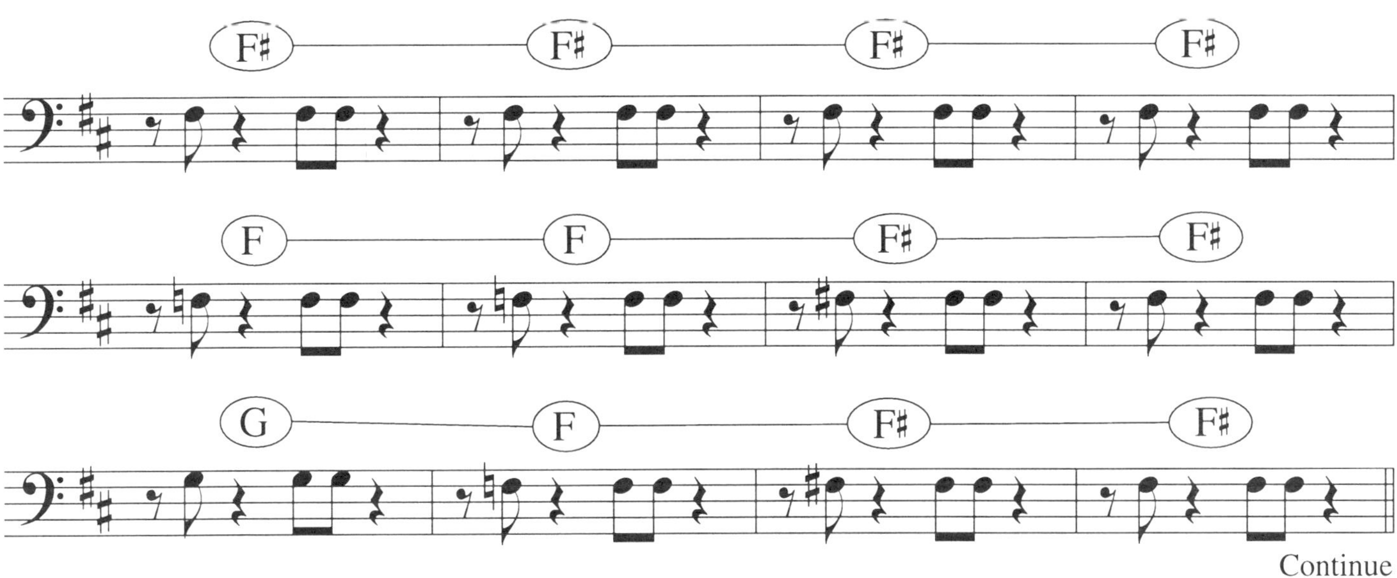

Continue

The scale we use to develop the inner melody into an improvised solo is D major with the seventh step lowered. In other words, we actually use G major's fingering, yet the root is D (D Mixolydian). More on this principle will be discussed in the next lesson. When the inner melody changes from F-sharp to F, we actually change to C major's fingering (G Mixolydian). For now, just focus on the inner melody.

Track # 27: To arrive at the D Mixolydian scale, start on D and count up to the seventh note, C-sharp, then lower it back to a C. Here is the basic scale:

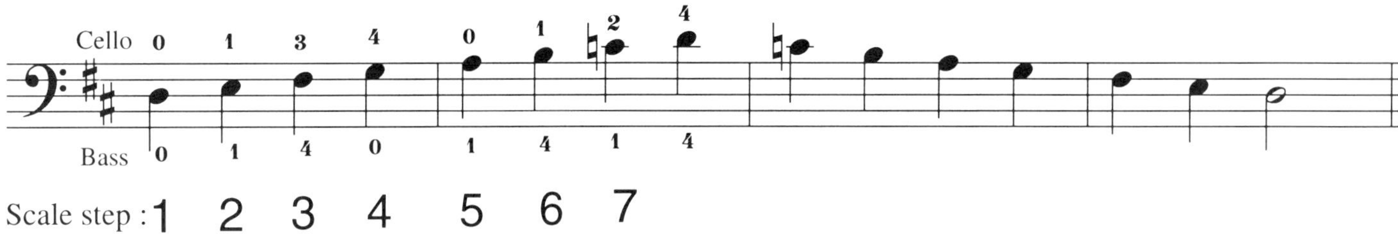

Cello 0 1 3 4 0 1 2 4
Bass 0 1 4 0 1 4 1 4
Scale step : 1 2 3 4 5 6 7

Track # 28: Now expand the inner melody to a short one-measure idea. We repeat the main idea 12 times yet incorporate the changing note. The first two choruses are written out. Try playing along with the third and fourth chorus on the CD learning the figure by ear.

1. chorus

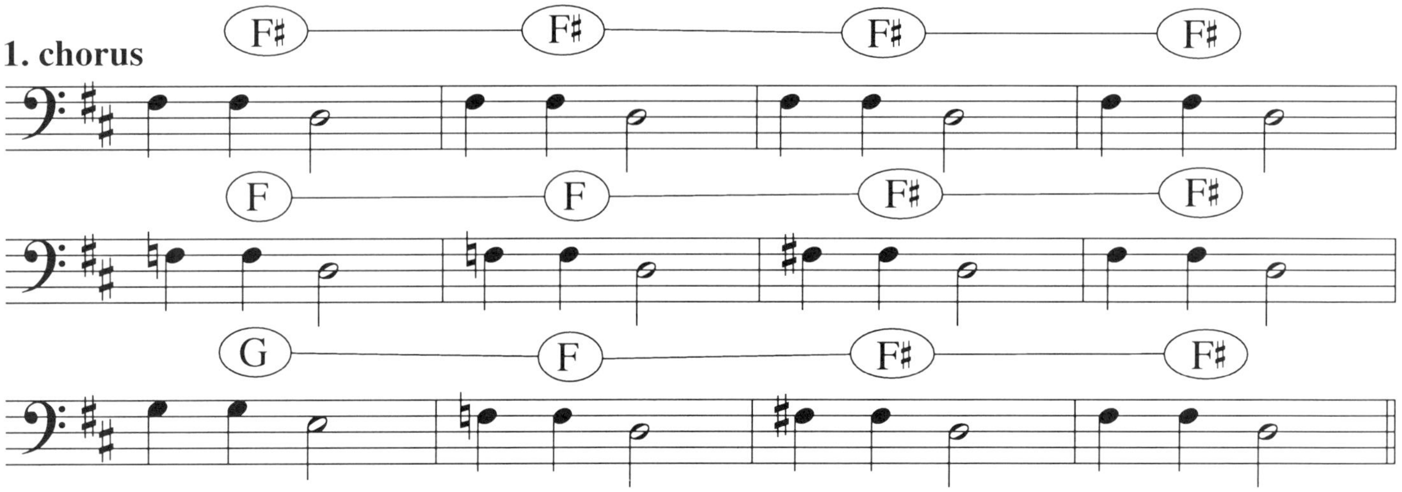

F♯ F♯ F♯ F♯
F F F♯ F♯
G F F♯ F♯

2. chorus

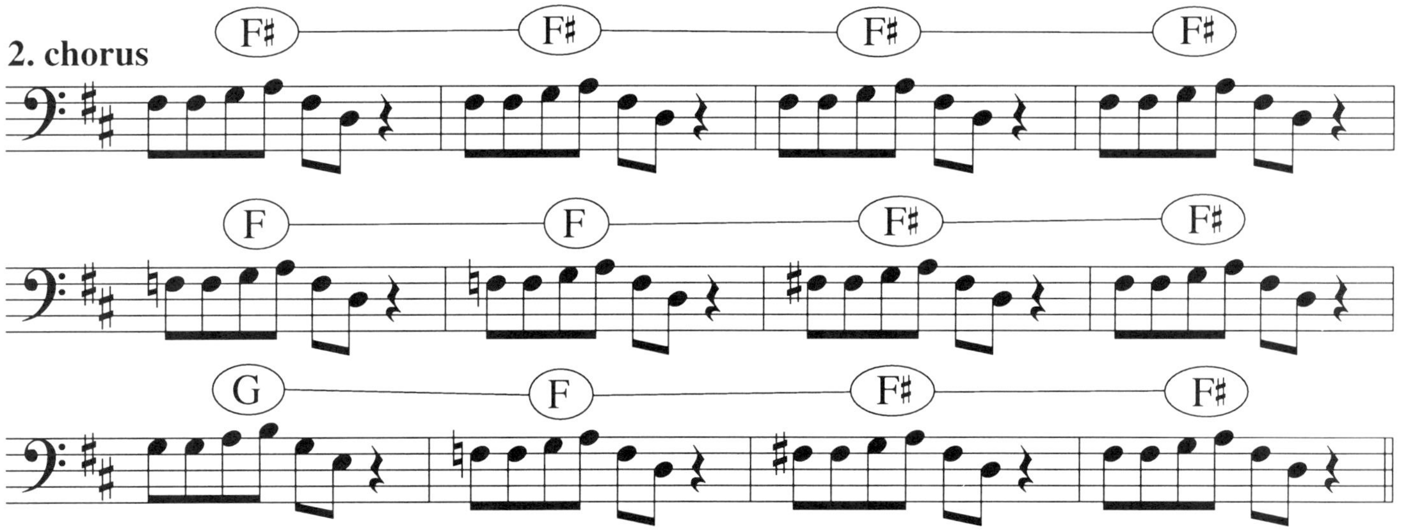

F♯ F♯ F♯ F♯
F F F♯ F♯
G F F♯ F♯

Play the next chorus by ear

Track # 29: This time make up your own one-measure figure, then repeat it being sure to adjust to the inner melody. Try to come up with a lick that incorporates the inner melody note. (Teacher: In a group setting, have one student play a lick and then see if the rest of the group is able to play the lick over the blues form adjusting the inner melody as demonstrated on Track # 28. Part of the group could simply play the inner melody itself to help others keep their place.)

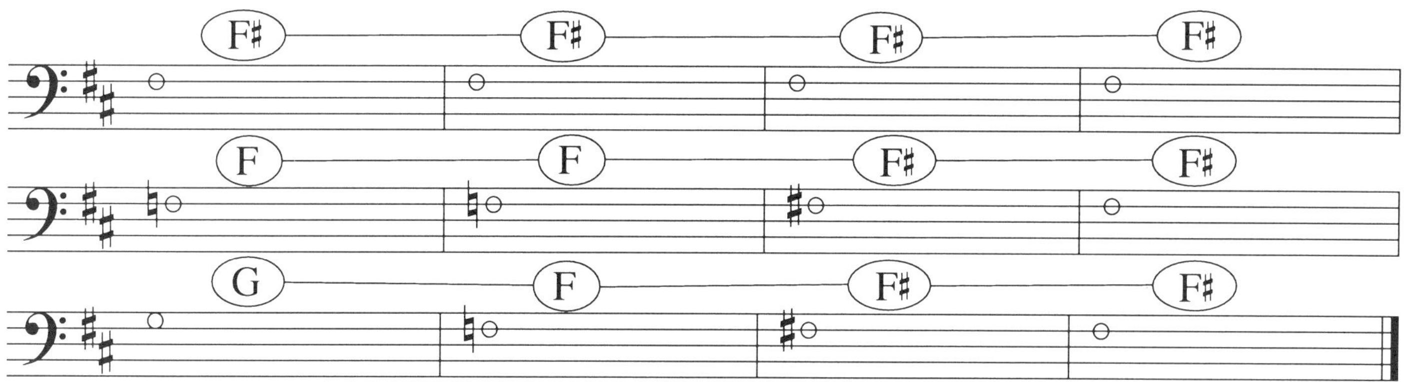

Track # 30: Let's expand the phrase to two measures. The inner melody is still the same. Again try to use the inner melody in the lick, however you don't have to play the inner melody note in every measure. The inner melody is only a guide you can follow if you like. If you don't play the inner melody, try to imagine it so you don't lose your place in the form. Feel free to change the figure in measures 9 and 10 because the inner melody suddenly changes in these measures. After the sample, make up your own two-measure lick and play it over the blues form:

1. chorus

F♯ F♯ F♯ F♯
F F F♯ F♯
G F F♯ F♯

2. chorus

F♯ F♯ F♯ F♯
F F F♯ F♯
G F F♯ F♯

Track # 31: Now try to improvise a four-measure phrase. You can repeat part of this in the second line. You are now welcome to play something completely new in the third line. Listen or play along with the sample, then improvise your own blues chorus:

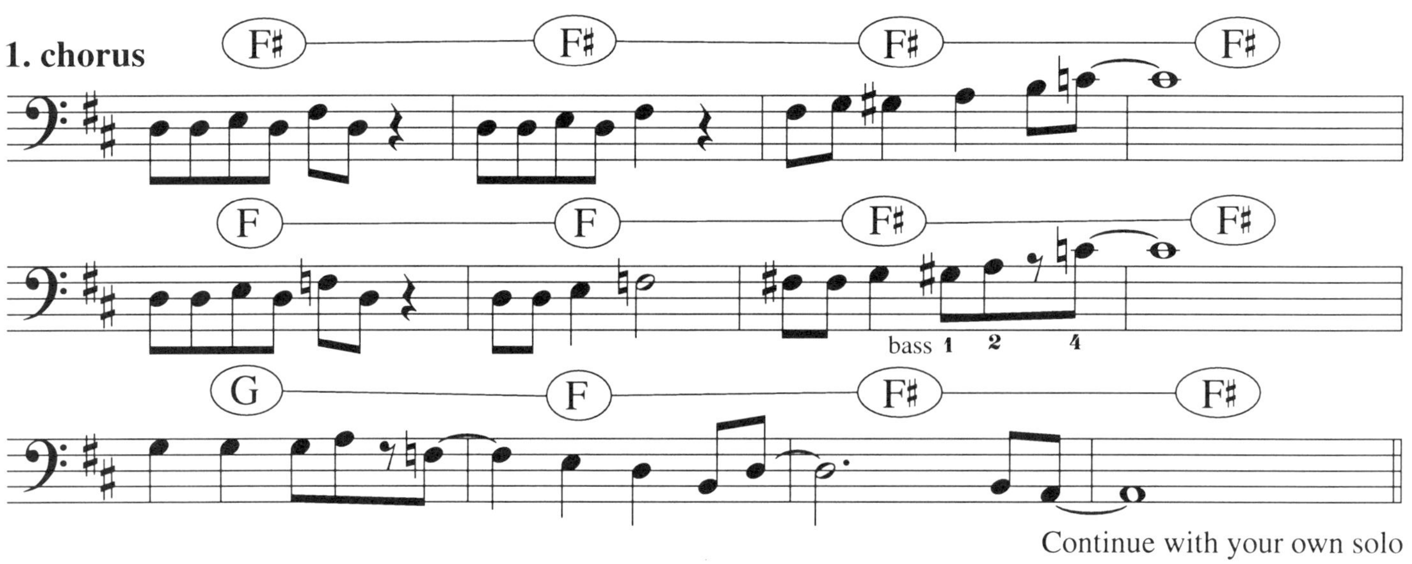

Track # 32: Here is a blues solo that more freely incorporates some of the ideas above. In addition, the solo incorporates story-telling principles from earlier lessons:

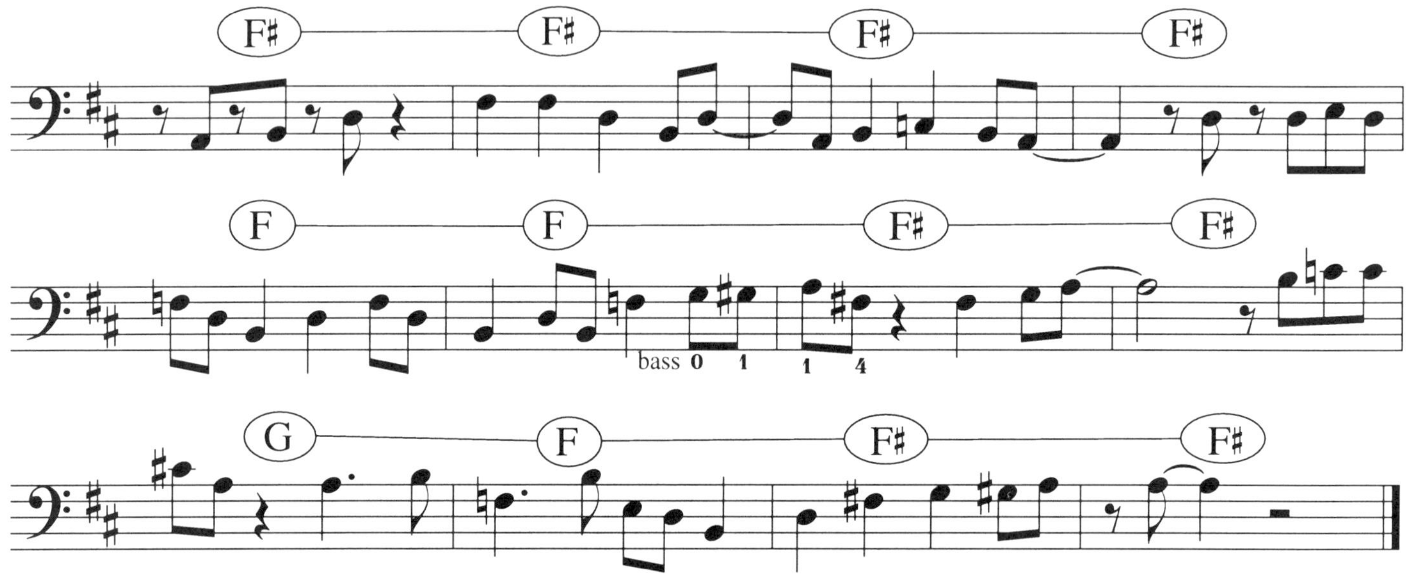

Track # 33: Go for it. As you improvise on the blues, try to keep your place in the form by hearing the inner melody in your head even if you don't actually play it. You may even want to review Lesson 2 (advanced) in Book 1. There we introduced a scale called the blues scale that works on the entire form even though it doesn't follow the inner melody. As you become a more accomplished improviser, you will learn that each "rule" represents a different approach, yet all the approaches are valid. In other words the more rules, the more approaches, the more possibilities. Listen to my solos on track # 34 to see if you can identify which approach I use where.

LESSON 4 (ADVANCED): HOW DID WE FIND THE INNER MELODIES ON THE BLUES?

The following is for advanced students who have been introduced to basic chord theory. You can easily play the solo on "Lazy Note Blues" without understanding the material below.

Just as in Lesson 3 (advanced), we find the inner melody by looking at the chords accompanying the blues. A traditional blues progression consists entirely of major chords with an added minor seventh. We start on the 3rd of the D7 chord, which then moves chromatically down to the 7th of the subdominant chord G7. In the last line, the 3rd of the D7 again moves to the 7th of the dominant A7 and the subdominant G7 then back to the 3rd of the tonic D7.

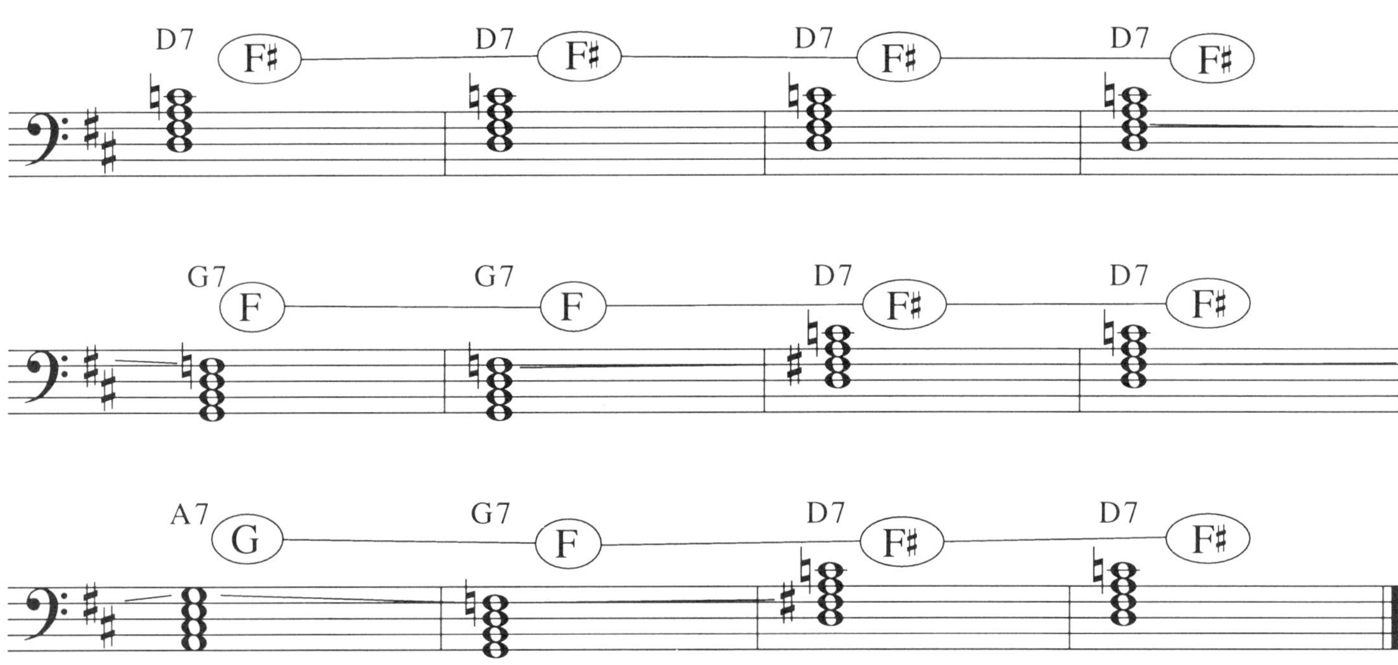

Exercise: Find another inner melody line for the blues by looking at the chords above. Remember to consider the chord notes in any octave:

D7 D7 D7 D7

G7 G7 D7 D7

A7 G7 D7 D7

Line A

LAZY NOTE BLUES

34 & 35

Blues Shuffle ♩ = 108

Cello opt.

M. Norgaard

5 · 17 · 29

p · *ff*

Solos

D7 D7 D7 D7 G7

G7 D7 D7 A7 G7 D7 D7

D7 D7 D7 D7 G7 G7

D7 D7 A7 G7 D7 D7

Last time D.S. al Coda

Line B

LAZY NOTE BLUES

Cello
(Line C)

LAZY NOTE BLUES

34 & 35

M. Norgaard

Bass

LAZY NOTE BLUES

34 & 35

Blues Shuffle ♩= 108

M. Norgaard

D7 D7 D7 D7 [5] D7 D7 D7

mf *pizz.*

8 D7 G7 G7 D7 D7 A7 G7

15 D7 D7 [17] 𝄋 D7 D7 D7 D7 G7

ff

22 G7 D7 D7 A7 G7 D7 D7

[29] D7 D7 D7 D7 G7 G7 D7

ff 3

36 D7 𝄌 A7 G7 D7 D7 **Solos** D7 D7

p

43 D7 D7 G7 G7 D7 D7 A7

50 G7 D7 D7 D7 D7 D7 D7

mf

57 G7 G7 D7 D7 A7 G7 D7 D7

Last time D.S. al Coda

65 𝄌 A7 G7 D7 D7 A7 G7 D7 D7 D7

ff

34 & 35

LAZY NOTE BLUES

Blues Shuffle ♩= 108

M. Norgaard

Line A
Line B
Line C
Bass
Piano

D7 D7 D7 D7 5 D7

6 D7 D7 D7 G7 G7

11 D7 D7 A7 G7 D7

A
B
C
Bass
Pia.
16
17
D7
ff
mp
21
G7
A7
26
29

A
B
C
Bass
Pia.
D7
G7
A7
Solos
optional accompaniment
vln
vla
p

A
B
C
Bass
Pia.
G7
D7
A7
mf

A
B
C
Bass
Pia.
A7
G7
D7
Last time D.S. al Coda
Last time D.S. al Coda
Last time D.S. al Coda
Last time D.S. al Coda
Last time D.S. al Coda
ff

LESSON 5:
AEOLIAN MINOR

In the previous lessons we learned how emphasizing different notes in the scale can change the way the phrase functions. A phrase emphasizing the root functions as an ending phrase, for example. In this lesson we will learn that by moving the root to another note on the major scale we create a whole new scale or mode. By moving the root to the sixth step of C major we create a scale called natural or Aeolian minor. Let's explore this scale using an underlying Latin rhythm.

Track # 36: First let's warm up with some Latin rhythms using straight eighths, as in Lesson 3. Try NOT to look at the music; just use your ear. Repeat the rhythm exactly as it is played on the CD. Use precise, even, short strokes with a slight accent.

To find the Aeolian minor, we count up to the sixth note in C major. Try counting both on the printed scale below and on your cello/bass using the C major finger pattern.

Track # 37: The note A becomes our new root. Say the scale degree numbers as you play the scale slowly:

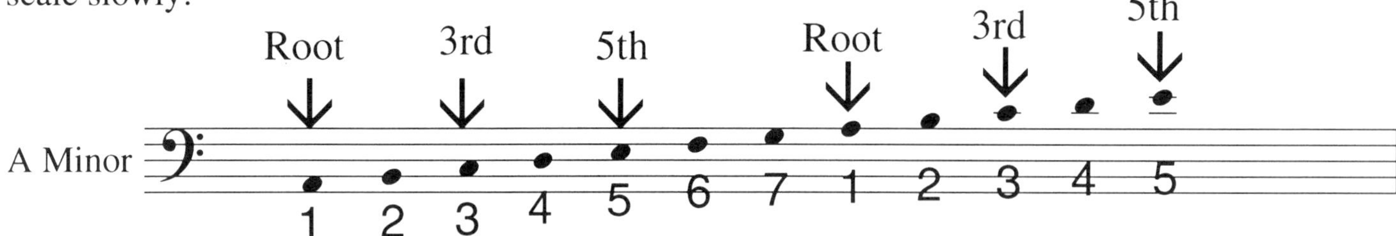

Track # 38: Play the scale using C major's fingering starting on A, first in quarter notes, then with rhythms. (Cellists: use the lower line if you are playing by yourself with Track # 44, which consists of rhythm section only.)

Cello & Bass (w/ CD)

Cello (solo)

Teacher

Piano continues ostinato

Track # 39: Answer the short question phrases below. Notice the figures start on the root (A) then the 3rd (C) then the 5th (E). Play the exercise two different ways:

a) Repeat the phrase (question) exactly as it is played on the CD.

b) Answer the question differently by improvising a short phrase that starts on the same note as the question phrase on the CD.

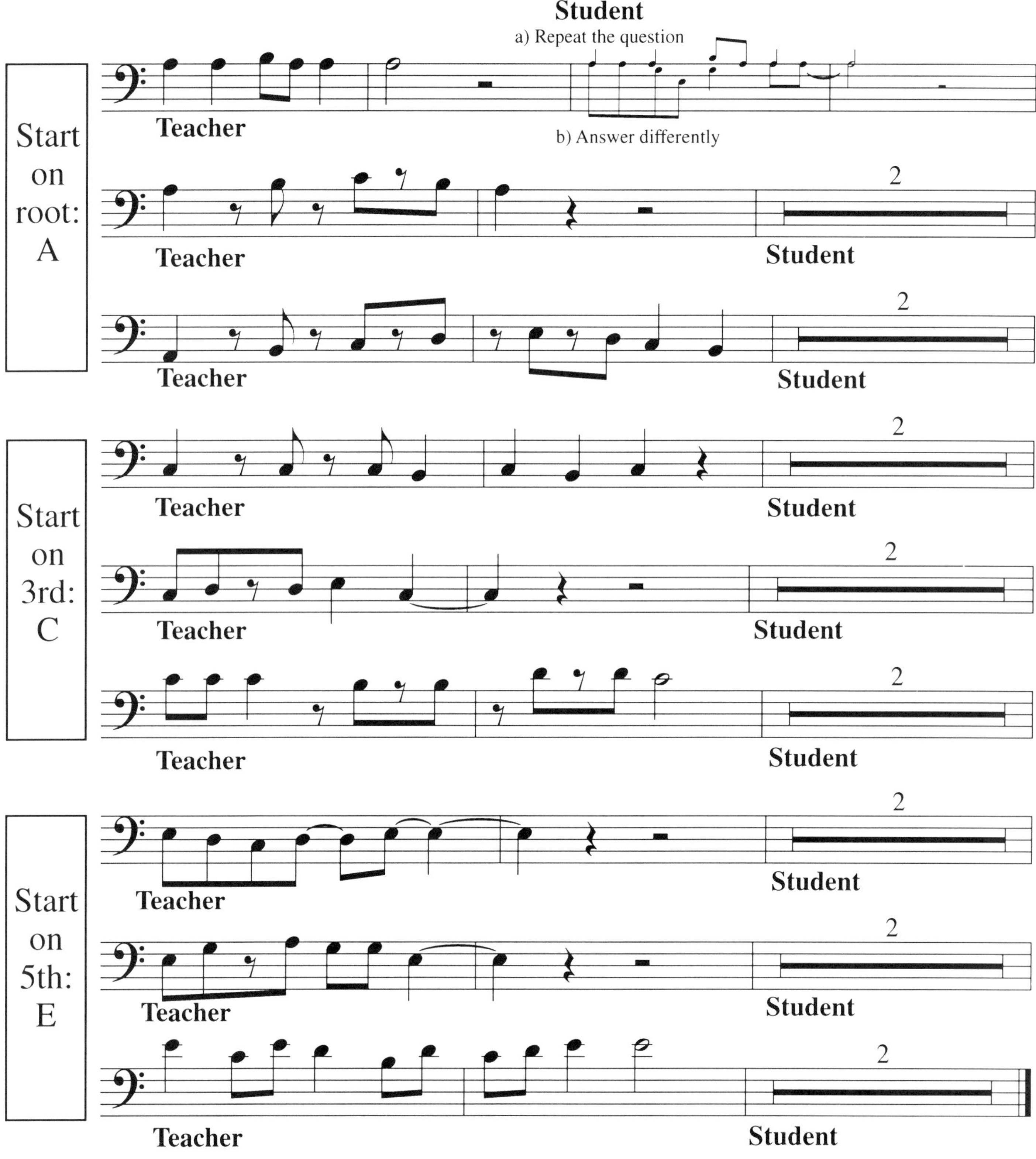

Track # 40: Let's divide the phrases into questions and answers as we did in Lesson 1. First answer the CD with a phrase that starts and ends on the root:

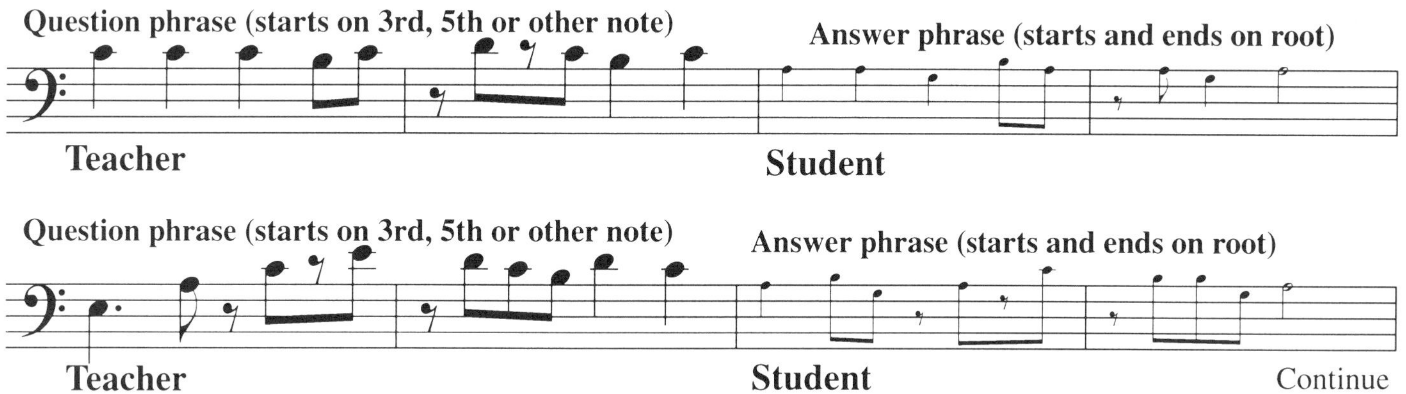

Track # 41: Now you ask the question by playing a short phrase that doesn't start or end on the root, and the CD will answer. You start:

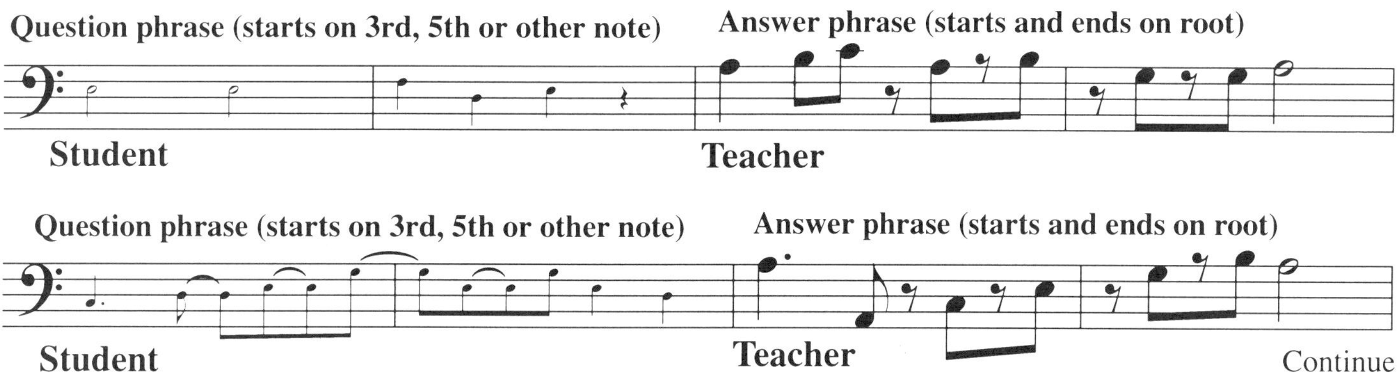

Track # 42: You should now be able to alternate between question and answer phrases within your own solo. After the CD sample, try it yourself. Remember, the round notes in your part are just to remind you to emphasize the root:

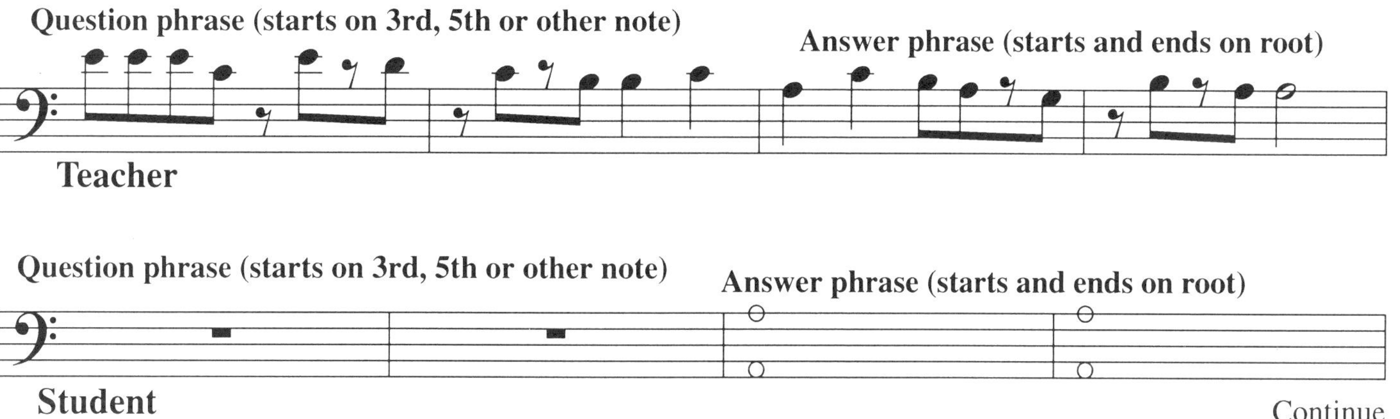

Track # 43: You should now be able to play the solo in "La Luna." Try to incorporate all of the elements we have studied in this book. Tell a story by starting slowly in a low register, then move up and start playing faster rhythms. Finally, end the solo with an answer phrase that emphasizes the root A. Here is the violin solo on the CD notated an octave down:

Track # 44: It's all yours. Here is a rhythm-section-only track you can use to practice the solo on "La Luna" many times. Try building a solo in which you really tell a story, building to a climax, and then resolve with an answer phrase. (Teacher: In a larger group have each student play a 16-measure solo roughly following the form below.)

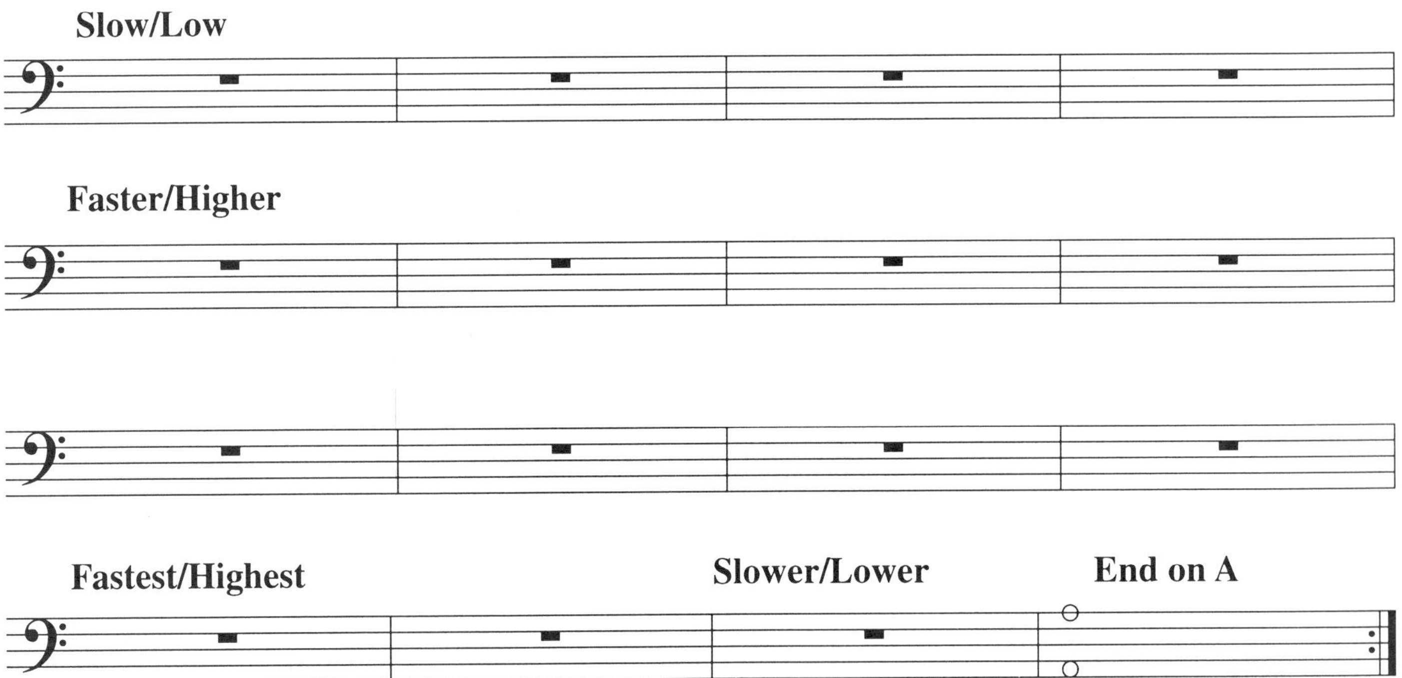

Line A

LA LUNA

45 & 46

Latin ♩= 145

Cello opt.

M. Norgaard

9

17

29

37

45

Solos

p optional accompaniment

Am Em Am Em Am Em Am Em Am Em Am Em Am Em Am Am

(CD repeats solo 4 times)

Last time D.C. al Coda

Line B

LA LUNA

45 & 46

Latin ♩= 145
Cello opt.

M. Norgaard

4 *mp* [9]

10

16 [17]

22 *ff*

28 [29] *f*

35 [37]

42 *ff* [45] *f*

48 **Solos** Am Em *p* optional accompaniment

55 Am Em Am Em Am Em

61 Am Em Am Em Am Em

67 Am Am (CD repeats solo 4 times) *ff* *Last time D.C. al Coda*

ff

Cello (Line C)

45 & 46

LA LUNA

Latin ♩= 145

M. Norgaard

mp sim.

9

17

ff

29

f

37

ff

45

f

Solos

Am Em Am Em Am Em Am

p optional accompaniment

Em Am Em Am Em Am Em

Am Am (CD repeats solo 4 times)

ff Last time D.C. al Coda

ff

Bass

LA LUNA

45 & 46

Latin ♩= 145

M. Norgaard

Am Em Am Em Am Em Am

pizz. *mp*

8 Em [9] Am Em Am A7 Dm E7

15 Am Em [17] Am Em Am A7 Dm

22 Dm Am Am Bm7♭5 E7 Am Am

ff

[29] G7 G7 Am Am G7 G7 Am Am

f

[37] G7 G7 Am Am Bm7♭5 E7 𝄌 Am Am

ff

[45] Am Em Am Em Am Em Am Am

f

Solos

53 Am Em Am Em Am Em Am

mf

60 Em Am Em Am Em Am Em

67 Am Am (CD repeats solo 4 times)

ff *Last time D.C. al Coda*

𝄌

ff

LA LUNA

45 & 46

Latin
♩ = 145
M. Norgaard
Line A
Line B
Line C
Bass
Piano
mp
pizz.
sim.
f
9
Am
Em
A7
Dm
E7
A
B
C
Pia.

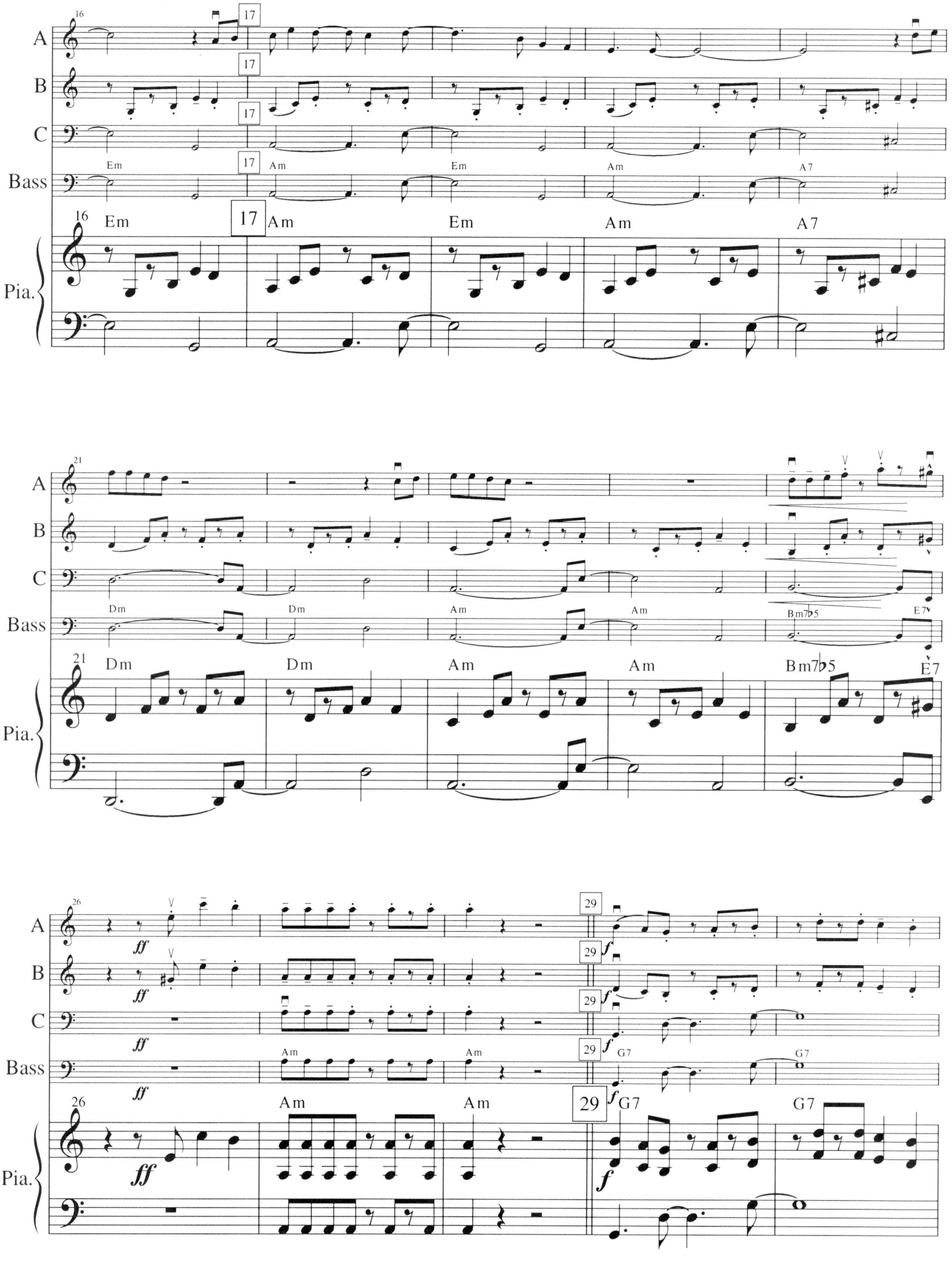

16 A B C Bass 17

Em Am Em Am A7

Pia.

21 A B C Bass

Dm Dm Am Am Bm7♭5 E7

Pia.

31
A
B
C
Bass
Am
G7
Pia.
36
37
41
Bm7♭5
E7
ff
45
f

46
A
B
C
Bass
Em
Am
Pia.
51
Solos
optional accompaniment
56

A
B
C
Bass
Pia.
Am
Em
ff
Last time D.C. al Coda
(CD repeats solo 4 times)

ABOUT THE AUTHOR

A performer, recording artist and educator, Martin Norgaard is currently a Doctoral Fellow in music education with a jazz emphasis at the University of Texas at Austin. Previously Norgaard was on the faculties of Belmont University's School of Music and Vanderbilt University's Blair School of Music. He leads his own jazz groups in New York, Nashville, and Austin, and has performed with artists as diverse as Rich McCready, Buddy Spicher, Sara Hickman, and Eliza Gilkyson. In addition to his *Jazz Fiddle Wizard* and *Jazz Fiddle Wizard Junior* books, Martin is the author of Mel Bay's transcriptions of Bonnie Rideout's Scottish fiddle record *Kindred Spirits,* Aubrey Haynie's *Doin' My Time,* Mel Bay's *French Tangos for Violin* and *The Greatest Stars of Bluegrass Music (fiddle edition).* One of Martin's own solos is transcribed in the *Fiddle 2000 Anthology,* also published by Mel Bay. After studying at the University of Copenhagen and the New England Conservatory, Martin earned his baccalaureate and master's degrees in jazz performance from William Paterson University in New Jersey and Queens College in New York, respectively.

In demand as a workshop clinician, Martin has taught or presented at the South Carolina Suzuki Institute, ASTA with NSOA National Conference and Studio Teachers Forum, Indiana Music Educators Association Conference, Georgia Music Educators Association Conference, California Music Educators Association Conference, International Association for Jazz Education Conference, Swing Week at Augusta Heritage Center, Music Educators National Conference, and Texas Music Educators Conference. As director of the Belmont Jazz String Quartet, he has appeared at the 2002 MENC National Conference, 2001 International Association for Jazz Education Conference, and 2001 Tennessee Music Educators Association Conference.

ABOUT THE EDITOR

Laura Reed has served as the editor of the *American String Teacher* journal of the American String Teachers Association with National School Orchestra Association and of the *American Music Teacher* journal of Music Teachers National Association. She currently teaches strings at Poplar Grove School in Franklin, Tennessee, near Nashville.

ABOUT JAZZ FIDDLE WIZARD JUNIOR BOOK 1

"Finally, we have an elementary-level method for strings focusing on jazz and blues. . . . I give it my highest and most enthusiastic recommendation."

Hollis Taylor, Fiddler Magazine, *Fall 2003*

"From the first exercise, the student is engaged in not only learning to play in the specified key, but to think for himself in developing skills to use the notes of the key in a solo. The logical progression of concept introduction is highly effective, especially with older middle school students. Jazz Fiddle Wizard Junior will certainly become a staple of the string student's jazz curriculum."

Kip Mason, American String Teacher, *August 2003*